DOCTOR·WHO

Winner Takes All

Collect all the exciting new Doctor Who *adventures:*

THE CLOCKWISE MAN
By Justin Richards

THE MONSTERS INSIDE
By Stephen Cole

DOCTOR·WHO

Winner Takes All

BY JACQUELINE RAYNER

BBC
BOOKS

3 5 7 9 10 8 6 4 2

Published in 2005 by BBC Books, an imprint of Ebury Publishing
Ebury Publishing is a division of the Random House Group

© Jacqueline Rayner 2005
Jacqueline Rayner has asserted her right to be identified as the author of this
Work in accordance with the Copyright, Designs and Patents Act 1988

Original series broadcast on BBC television
Format © BBC 1963
'Doctor Who', 'TARDIS' and the Doctor Who logo are trademarks of the
British Broadcasting Corporation and are used under licence.

The Random House Group Limited Reg. No. 954009
Addresses for companies within the Random House Group can be found at
www.randomhouse.co.uk

A CIP catalogue record for this book is available from the British Library

ISBN-13: 9781849907156

Commissioning Editors: Shirley Patton/Stuart Cooper
Creative Director and Editor: Justin Richards
Production Controller: Alenka Oblak

Doctor Who is a BBC Wales production for BBC ONE
Executive Producers: Russell T Davies, Julie Gardner and Mal Young
Producer: Phil Collinson

This book is a work of fiction. Names, characters, places and
incidents are either a product of the author's imagination or
used fictitiously. Any resemblance to actual people living
or dead, events or locales is entirely coincidental.

Cover design by Henry Steadman © BBC 2005
Typeset in Albertina by Rocket Editorial, Aylesbury, Bucks

Printed and bound in the USA

For Nick

'I thought I'd better call home,' said Rose, wandering into the TARDIS's huge, vaulted control room and waving her phone at the Doctor.

The Doctor had his arms crossed and was leaning with his back against a wall, staring across at the large, circular structure that sat in the centre of the room, on which a myriad of lights flickered and sparkled. His face shone green in the glow from a tall, thin column in the centre of the structure which indicated that they were in flight. Rose didn't know where they were going, but perhaps the Doctor could tell from observing these things exactly where in the universe the time-and-space machine was taking them. He nodded at her. She felt slightly cheated, having geared herself up for – well, not an argument, just that flicker of displeasure that occasionally crossed his face when she mentioned family.

She pushed a bit further. 'It's just that my mum'll worry. You know that my mum'll worry. And I did promise. Sort of.'

He nodded again. 'And you think she'll worry less if you tell her you've been out facing aliens but at the moment you're just spinning through the space-time vortex.'

Rose frowned. 'She'll worry less if she thinks I'm not dead!'

The Doctor – her best friend, the Doctor, who outwardly seemed to be a striking, forty-ish human with a soft northern accent, but was, she knew, actually a 900-year-old alien from some galaxy far, far away – could be a bit dismissive of her mum's worries sometimes. She wasn't sure if it was something to do with not being human, or just something to do with being the Doctor. She didn't even know if he'd ever had a mum of his own. If you didn't understand mums in general, there was no way you'd get Jackie Tyler.

'I'll just give her a quick call. Well, I say quick, she'll keep me on for hours, wanting to know everything – she can talk for England, my mum can. Hope you weren't planning to stop off at any planets this morning.'

He grinned. 'My planet-hopping can wait till this afternoon.'

She smiled back, and pressed the speed-dial button that called her mum. She just had to accept that, through the Doctor's genius, her ordinary mobile could now transcend space and time; if she thought about it too much her mind began to feel like it was overheating.

The phone rang six times before it was picked up, which surprised Rose. Her mum loved nothing better than a good old natter, and the phone was usually snatched up when it had barely got out its first *brring*. 'Hiya, Mum,' she said.

The voice at the other end was exuberant. 'Rose! What are you doing? Where are you?' Then a slight pause. 'Are you still with him?'

Rose smiled. 'I'm just hanging around in the time machine. And yeah, I'm still with him.'

The Doctor looked up at this and did a sarky wave that she knew was directed at Jackie. Rose waved back happily. 'Mum says hi,' she said, with her hand over the phone.

'And are you planning on coming home any time soon?' Jackie was saying. 'Everyone misses you. Mickey misses you. I miss you. You know, one of these days you'll decide to come home and it'll be too late, I won't be here any more.'

Rose sighed. 'Don't be silly, Mum. I'll pop back for a visit soon. Make sure the family silver gets a good polish ready.'

'Family silver!' Rose could hear Jackie's voice go up a notch. 'It might please you to joke, my girl, but I'll have you know that I've just won the lottery.'

'You what?' Rose said. 'That's incredible! I don't believe it! How much?'

There was a sound, somewhere outside Jackie's end of the phone call. A shout, or a cry, or something. 'Listen love, I've got to go now. Lovely to hear from you. Gotta go.'

There was a click, and the phone was silent. Rose looked down at it in surprise. Then, shaking her head, she slipped the phone back in her pocket.

'Talk for England, you said,' the Doctor commented, strolling over to the central controls. 'Can't get her off the phone.'

'My mum's won the lottery!' Rose started pacing around

the control room, her eyes shining. 'How brilliant is that? We'll be able to get a great big house –'

The Doctor raised an eyebrow, gesturing at the enormous room in which they stood.

'– go on holiday – the Caribbean or somewhere – or Florida!'

The Doctor stared at her. 'I can take you anywhere in time and space!'

She wasn't listening. 'I've always wanted to go to Disney-land.'

'Yeah, brilliant, grown men dressed up as mice and kids being sick on roller coasters. I can take you to planets where there are *real* talking mice. And ducks!'

She shrugged. 'But you haven't, though, have you? And you wouldn't take my mum, anyway.'

He grinned. 'Well, maybe not. Don't wanna scare the mice.' He carried on before Rose could respond. 'She all happy then, is she? Too busy spending to talk to you?'

Rose grimaced. 'Yeah, that was weird.' She paused for a second, and then gave him what she hoped was a winning smile. 'Don't s'pose we could pop home for a bit, could we? Just to check on her.'

'D'you think something's up?' he asked.

'No, not really. But she did say something about not being there when I get back,' Rose said. 'Don't want to turn up one day and find she's gone off to some country mansion and chucked out all my stuff.'

'A couple of old posters and a teddy bear? Yeah, that'd be a tragedy.'

Rose gave him a mock glare. 'I'm nineteen years old, I think I have grown out of teddy bears, and I do have a few more possessions than that. Some of which have sentimental value, I'll have you know. So could we go home please? Just for a flying visit, I promise.'

'Yeah, all right.' He nodded, and started setting a course. 'I don't know, humans, always come with so much baggage…'

'Yeah, it's a crime, isn't it?' she agreed. And then, after a moment. 'You don't really think she'd chuck out Mr Tedopoulos, do you?'

The Doctor just grinned.

ONE

The TARDIS landed in a courtyard on the Powell Estate. Rose popped her head out of the doorway, saw the Chinese takeaway in front of her, the library and youth club over to one side, and realised that the time machine had come back to its favourite spot; it'd landed here before.

She stepped out of the spaceship. On the outside it looked like a tall blue box, an old-fashioned police box – big enough in its way, big enough to fit in five or six people, if they were prepared to be quite friendly, but not big enough to fit in an enormous control room and all the other bits that formed the inside of the TARDIS. She'd come to accept it – funny how quickly you got used to even the most incredible things – but it was something else that her mind didn't really like to dwell on, not the ins and outs and hows and whys of it all.

There to her right was Bucknall House, and there, if she squinted upwards, was number 48. Home. Or was it?

She turned back to the blue box. Well, no one said you couldn't have more than one home.

Rose had still got a key, but as the two of them climbed up the concrete steps towards the flat she wondered if she should really use it. Key out of her pocket, look at it, put it back in, take it out again, look at it… It wasn't as if her mum was expecting her, and she didn't want to catch her out. If Jackie had won the lottery the champagne would have been flowing a bit, and goodness knows what state the flat – and Jackie – would be in by now.

She hesitated for a moment on the walkway outside the front door, key in her hand. Then she knocked on the door.

After a moment it opened on the chain, which Rose thought a bit odd, but forgot it almost at once when she saw her mum, petite and blonde just like Rose herself, peering through the gap. The chain came off immediately, and the door had barely swung open when Jackie had her arms round Rose. 'You're here! You're here!'

Rose grinned as she hugged her mum back. 'Yeah, looks like it.'

Jackie looked at her accusingly as she came out of the embrace. 'But don't tell me, you're not stopping.'

'Oh, we'll hang around for the party,' Rose said.

'The party? I'm expected to throw a party every time you turn up on the doorstep?'

'No, Mum,' said Rose, following her into the flat, 'the party cos you've won the lottery.'

Jackie gave a snort of laughter, turning to look back at

the doorway. 'That? I just won some games thing. You know, on the scratchcards. Gave it to Mickey.' She peered over Rose's shoulder. 'Come on, where's his nibs then? Doesn't he want a cup of tea?'

The Doctor appeared in the doorway, grinning. 'Just waiting to be asked in.'

'He needs to be asked in,' Rose said to her mum. 'Like a vampire does.'

Jackie looked as if she believed it, as if she thought the Doctor might turn into a bat any minute.

'Not really,' Rose added. 'Shall we have that cup of tea, then?'

'So, what's this scratchcard thing?' Rose asked after a bit, when they were settled comfortably on the white leather chairs in the lounge, and on to their second cup each.

Jackie leaned over to grab hold of her bag. She put in a hand and pulled out a sheaf of bits of orange cardboard. Rose took a couple. They all had a picture of a cartoon animal on them, with a giant speech bubble coming out of its mouth. The speech bubble had bits of silvery stuff on it, with 'Sorry, you've not won this time! Please try again!' showing through on the card underneath, where the silver had been scratched off.

'What's that, a hedgehog?' said Rose, indicating the cartoon animal.

'Percy the Porcupine,' said Jackie. 'It's this character they're using. Test promotion in this area. Every time you buy something down the town, you get one of these cards.

Then you go to a little booth where there's some poor out-of-work student dressed as a porcupine, and they give you your prize. Daft thing is, they didn't even think to limit the number of cards you can get! If you get all your shopping a bit at a time, you can get dozens of the things. I got eight by breaking up a bag of carrots the other day.'

'Oh, Mum!' said Rose, part embarrassed, part reluctantly proud.

Jackie sniffed. 'Don't you "oh, Mum" me. It's not like I've got a lot to look forward to, my only daughter off gallivanting round the galaxy and me all alone here. Big prize is a holiday, and I couldn't half do with that. Sun, sand, men in little shorts…'

'Talking mice?' Rose muttered under her breath. But Jackie wasn't listening.

'Mrs Hall down the road won one, it's wasted on someone like that, you know what she's like, probably won't take her hat and coat off even if it's eighty degrees, and there's me with a bikini still with its label on stuck in the drawer that I've never had a chance to wear…'

'Oh, Mum!' said Rose again.

'Nothing like getting something for nothing, is there?' put in the Doctor.

'And what's wrong with that, I'd like to know,' said Jackie, bristling.

'Nothing. That's what I said.' The Doctor took the cards from Rose and examined them. 'Just odd, don't you think, they don't seem to be promoting anything in particular. Beware porcupines bearing gifts, an' all that.'

Rose took back the cards and handed them to her mum. 'It's a test thing, ain't it? They'll do the proper promoting when it's all over the country or whatever. Or maybe they just want people to spend more money at the shops. What, d'you think it's really aliens, trying to take over the world with free holidays and games consoles?'

'Yeah, well, it could happen,' said the Doctor. He got up and wandered out of the room.

'Don't mind us!' Jackie called after him. 'Make yourself at home!'

'I will, ta,' the Doctor's voice came back.

Rose turned back to Jackie. 'Glad you're not moving to a country mansion, though.'

'What?'

'I thought you'd won the lottery, remember.'

Jackie sighed. 'Wish I had. Wish I was getting out of this place.' She looked genuinely down for a moment.

Rose stared. 'But you love this place! All your friends are here and everything!'

Jackie shrugged. 'It's gone downhill since you left, sweetheart. Do you remember that Darren Pye? Went to your school.'

Rose thought for a second, and then shuddered. 'Two years above me. Looked like a shaved gorilla only not as handsome. Hardly ever turned up, and when he did the police were usually not far behind him. Thumped kids for their lunch money, only he didn't stop with lunch money, and he didn't stop with thumping, either.'

'He's moved in two down three across,' said Jackie.

Rose tried to picture which flat she meant. 'What happened to Mrs McGregor?'

'Started wandering about the streets in her nightie, thought it was still the war. That Tony of hers put her in a home down Sydenham way.'

'And the council put in Darren Pye?'

'They put in Mrs Pye, which means you get Darren.' Jackie shuddered. 'It was when you phoned, he'd been having a go at that Jade, took her purse and her mobile – and she won't call the police, he said he'd have her if she did – wouldn't let her down the stairs, and she thought he was going to push her down them, and she's due any day – I had to go to her, she was crying so much I thought she'd have the baby then and there, and you read in the papers how long it takes ambulances to get here these days.' She paused, half worried, half indignant. 'She was that scared, I gave her my phone so she can call for help if she needs it, and I don't begrudge her although I'll miss it till I get it back and I hope she's not answering calls meant for me... I know it's not like aliens and that, and he's not even really hurt anyone yet, and it's not like he's trying to take over the world, but...'

The Doctor wandered back in then, hands behind his back, and leapt on this.

'Yeah, aliens trying to take over the world usually have a better motive than just wanting to make people's lives a misery.'

Rose looked at the Doctor. 'So, are we gonna sort him out then?'

The Doctor looked at her in mock surprise. 'I never save anything smaller than a planet.' He grinned, and pulled his hands out from behind his back. He was holding something blue and furry. 'Oh, and sometimes a teddy bear.'

She grabbed the furry object. 'Mr Tedopoulos!' Then she thought for a second, and used the bear to whack him across the chest. 'You went in my bedroom?'

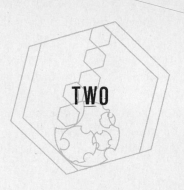

TWO

Rose thought they'd better go and see Mickey while they were there, because he'd never forgive her if they didn't, or so Jackie said, and Rose thought she was probably right. After all, it wasn't as if they'd ever even formally split up. But long-distance relationships were bad enough when one person went off to college, or got a job further than the end of a tube line; when someone was commuting from London to the end of the world, or to Victorian times or something, they didn't really stand much chance at all.

Mickey didn't seem particularly surprised to see them, and Rose guessed – which Mickey confirmed – that her mum had been on the phone the instant they left the flat. She looked at him, and felt an unexpected wave of affection surge through her. With his gorgeous dark skin and twinkling eyes, he really had been a bit of a catch. Didn't have a time machine, of course, but even so...

But that was her old life, and she wasn't that person any more.

'Hope we're not interrupting anything,' she said.

'Just playing a game, babe,' he said.

'And you're how old? Six?' said the Doctor. 'Nice bit of Snakes and Ladders, is it, or something a bit more sophisticated like Snap?'

Mickey didn't seem to take offence. 'This games thing that Rose's mum got me. Thought it was a bit of a rip-off at first, not a PlayStation or an Xbox or anything and you only get one game, but it's brilliant. You'd like it. All aliens and stuff.'

The Doctor seemed unconvinced.

'Come on, I'll show you,' Mickey said.

The Doctor had dragged a second chair up close to the TV, and Rose was perched on its arm. There was a pile of games on the floor: *Gran Turismo*, *Resident Evil*, *Bad Wolf*, *TimeSplitters 2*, loads of football stuff. She'd picked up the top one and was examining it: an orange cardboard box that had a picture of a cartoon porcupine shooting a cartoon insect-thing on it. Big black letters gave the game's name: *Death to Mantodeans*. The two men were discussing the game itself, passing the control pad between chairs, across Rose. She might have been a cushion for all the notice they were taking of her.

'Smart graphics,' said the Doctor.

'Yeah, first-person's cool, innit?' said Mickey. 'All *Blair Witchy*, like you really feel you're there, yeah? And it's never the same twice. The amount of variables they must've programmed in is amazing.'

'And it's got these porcupines in it, has it?' said Rose, trying to take part in the conversation. It wasn't as if she couldn't have been really good at this stuff herself if she'd wanted to be, but she just couldn't see the point. 'The ones from the promotion?'

'Yeah, right at the beginning,' Mickey said. 'They're at war with these other things called Mantodeans, like giant praying mantises sort of thing, and they send you off on a mission to infiltrate the enemy stronghold. That's what it's all about. 'Spect they'll pop up again at the end if you win. No one's done it yet, though.'

'How d'you know?' Rose asked.

'Cos I have my finger on the pulse, babe.'

She kept looking enquiringly at him till he continued. 'They're offering a prize. First person to complete the game gets a load of cash. So everyone round here wants to give it a go. Nag at their mums till they win a game off the shopping. Set up a message board on the net an' that, talking about it. Hardly anyone's even got past the training level.'

'Training level?' said the Doctor.

'Yeah, that's what they call it. It's all cartoony, not like this stuff.' He indicated the screen, which currently showed a realistic-looking view of a tunnel entrance. 'All tests and that. If it wasn't for the prize, I reckon a lot of people would've given up. But once you've done it, you get this intro about the proper game, the mission, and you get to play the good stuff.'

'And not many people have got that far then?' asked

Rose, pretending interest just for something to say.

'Nah. Hardly any, I reckon. So just call me da man and get ready to worship at my feet, cos that prize is gonna be mine.'

The Doctor pointed at an indicator in the corner of the screen. The score wasn't very high. 'Yeah, looks like you're on the home stretch, da man.'

Mickey got all defensive. 'Yeah, well, no one's got very far yet. Reckon there's a glitch or something. Half the time it doesn't save your game and you have to go back to the beginning. And the puzzles you gotta work out, they're like mega brainy stuff. Maths and that.'

'Puzzles?' said the Doctor.

Mickey reached across Rose for the controller, and pressed down on a button. On the TV screen, Rose watched a shaky corridor rush past. At the end was an imposing-looking door. A panel on the door came into focus, with numbers and letters scrolling across it.

The Doctor sat up. 'I'm surprised anyone's got past this at all. Look at the algorithms on that!'

Mickey grinned. 'Ladies present!'

The Doctor leaned across Rose and took the controller off Mickey.

'There's all sorts of different ones,' Mickey said help-fully. 'Some are sort of, you know, pictogrammy things. Or odd ones out, that sort of thing.'

The Doctor was already staring at the screen, mutter-ing things like, 'Convert that section to binary... If d equals 8.9 to the power of y... Ha ha!' With a triumphant yell he stabbed at the controls. On the screen, the door slid open.

'Watch out!' called Mickey. 'They're the bad guys! The Mantodeans.'

On the other side of the door there was a cluster of monsters, which were, as Mickey had said, like giant green praying mantises. They stood upright on stick-thin legs and had terrifying pincer-like jaws that they began to snap together as they approached the door – it looked as if they were heading straight for the screen, as if they'd come out into Mickey's living room if they didn't stop.

'Do I have any weapons?' asked the Doctor.

'Arrow keys to aim, red button to fire,' said Mickey.

On the screen, the monsters shrieked one by one, as each fell in a blaze of laser beams.

'You don't like guns,' said Rose critically.

'I hate guns,' replied the Doctor. 'Which isn't to say that a bit of fantasy violence can't be therapeutic. Now, here's the next door… Will there be any more Mantodeans the other side, I wonder?'

'Yeah, probably,' said Mickey. 'Only now they know you're there, they won't be so easy to get. First couple of times I did this, I got my head bitten off.'

'Brilliant!' said the Doctor.

Mickey leaned forward and looked across at him. 'Come off it, you do this stuff for real! What's so exciting about playing a game?'

The Doctor leaned back on his chair. 'Yeah, well, the thing about games as opposed to real life is, one, you're

honing your reflexes, right, two, you're practising strat-
egic thinking, and three, you've usually got a cup of tea
and a packet of HobNobs at hand.'

'And four, real aliens aren't trying to bite your head off,
right?'

The Doctor grinned. 'Yeah, I s'pose there's a downside
as well. So, about that cuppa then...'

'You just had two cups at my mum's,' said Rose. 'And
three sandwiches and two cakes.'

'Don't tell me England's got a tea-restriction law these
days,' the Doctor said. 'If it has, I'll probably have to take
down the government. Again.'

Mickey shrugged. 'Whatever, the milk's probably off,
and there won't be any biscuits.'

'Not since I stopped doing your shopping for you,'
Rose put it.

He bridled. 'I never asked you to do my shopping!'

She nodded. 'You're right. You never asked. You just
gazed at me like a hungry puppy till I felt sorry for you.'

Mickey grinned and fluttered his eyelashes. 'Woof
woof.'

Not looking up from the screen, the Doctor said,
'There's some cash in my pocket. Go and get us some
milk and biscuits, will you, Rose? Oh, and some Winalot
for the Jack Russell over there.'

With an affected sigh, Rose helped herself to a handful
of change from the pocket of his battered leather jacket,
weeding out a couple of Roman sesterces and a £10 coin
which claimed to show the head of William V.

She slid off the chair arm, nearly tripping over the wires that connected the control pad to the games console. 'Don't miss me too much,' she said.

The Doctor kept his eyes on the screen. 'Missing you already,' he said.

THREE

Rose could see down to the shop from the walkway by Mickey's flat. There was hardly anyone around. Maybe they were all indoors playing computer games, like Mickey, hoping to win the prize. Or maybe they'd seen Darren Pye leaning against the wall and decided to steer clear.

She recognised him at once, even though she hadn't seen him since he left school – well, since he stopped coming to school – and that was years ago. She'd attracted his attention a few times, because if you were an individual and stood up for things and refused to be a victim, then some people wanted to make you into a victim. But it'd never been bad, not like it had for some.

And she wasn't going to let a thug like that stop her from going to the shop. She walked down the stairs, out into the courtyard. She virtually saw his ears prick up as her footsteps sounded, and he lazily swung his head round.

'Oi! Oi, you!'

She ignored him, kept walking past.

'I'm talking to you, slag.'

Ignored him.

'Oi, slag, heard your boyfriend done you in.'

So he knew who she was. 'Don't believe everything you read in the *Beano*,' she called back. She'd faced aliens and goodness knows what; she wasn't going to let an immature thug get to her. It was surprisingly easy. Sticks and stones, she thought.

'Thought it ran in families,' he said. 'I heard your slag of a mother did in her husband.'

That made her flush with anger, anger for her mother and her long-dead father, but then she thought again about the aliens she'd faced, and imagined Darren Pye wetting himself if he came face to face with the Nestene Consciousness or something, and that made her smile instead.

She went into the shop and browsed the shelves, picking up a two-pinter of semi-skimmed, a packet of custard creams and, to be on the safe side, a box of teabags as well. 'Thanks,' she said to Maureen behind the counter, as everything went into a blue plastic bag. 'Do I get one of them scratchcards, then?'

Maureen snorted. 'No you don't. Bloomin' things. Everyone's going down the road just so as they can get some stupid prize, even if they only want a loaf of bread. I know mine might be a few pence dearer, but it's £1.20 bus fare on top, which makes my bread a lot cheaper overall, and you can just tell your mum that, young Rose.'

Rose laughed. 'Come off it, like she'd listen! Any chance of something for nothing and my mum'll be in there, and she's got a bus pass anyway.' She picked up the carrier bag and smiled a farewell.

And she was just turning to leave when she heard the cry. It was the sound of someone in pain, and it was followed by laughter.

She'd never been the sort of person who hesitated when someone was in trouble – mistakenly, sometimes, 'Rose jumps in with both feet,' her mum had said, sometimes proudly, more often pityingly.

So she ran out of the shop, towards the cry. Not that she had to go far: there was Mrs Desai right in front of her, both hands clutched to her temples as if warding off a blow. There was a little trickle of blood just creeping between her fingers, and behind her Darren Pye had picked up another stone ready to throw. Sticks and stones, she thought again. They hurt.

Rose launched herself at him. It wasn't sensible, and it certainly didn't fit in with her policy of ignoring him, but she did it anyway. 'Don't you dare!' she yelled. 'Don't you dare!' She swung the blue carrier bag at him. He dropped the stone, and there was a satisfying 'whumph' as the plastic bottle of milk split on impact, showering him with white droplets. He shook it out of his hair like a dog.

'Big mistake,' he said to her, grabbing her by the hood of her top and yanking her off balance. 'Little girl wants to be a hero.

She twisted out of his grasp. 'I've dealt with a lot bigger

than you. Not uglier, though, and that's saying plenty if you've ever seen a Slitheen.'

Darren gave her a shove. 'Bigger mistake.' And he pulled out a knife.

For a split second, Rose could see nothing but the knife.

Then a leather-clad arm descended over Darren's shoulder and twisted his wrist, and the knife clattered to the ground. 'Naughty naughty,' said the Doctor, shoving Darren away. The lad stumbled a few steps, then caught his balance and picked up the knife again. The Doctor stood his ground, strong and imposing. 'Really wanna risk it?'

To Rose's relief, Darren thought better of it. He glared at them both, but then turned and swaggered off, milk still dribbling down his neck.

Once he was round the corner, out of sight, the Doctor turned to Rose. 'And you thought it was a good idea to take on, single-handedly, someone who's twice your size and carrying a knife,' he said.

She shrugged, torn between relief, embarrassment and bravado. 'Seemed like a good idea at the time.'

He glanced down at the dripping carrier bag. 'You've got a lotta bottle, I'll say that for you.'

'Just call me the dairy avenger.'

'Queen of the cream.'

She grinned. 'They'll do me for assault and buttery.'

Mrs Desai and Maureen came out of the shop, from where they'd clearly been watching the show. 'Good on

yer, Rose,' called out Maureen. Mrs Desai waved her shy
thanks.

'I'd go get that checked out in casualty if I were you,
Mrs Desai,' Rose called back.

'No, you wouldn't,' whispered the Doctor in an aside.
'You'd carry on like a brave little soldier.'

She threw him a withering look. 'What are you doing
out here anyway? Did your biscuit cravings get the better
of you?' She pulled the milk-sodden, now-crushed packet
of custard creams out of the bag and waved it in his face.
He took it, opened it and put a whole one in his mouth.

'My fpider fenfe waf tingling,' he said round a mouth-
ful of crumbs and cream filling.

'Be serious,' she said. 'And it's rude to talk with your
mouth full.'

He swallowed the biscuit. 'I'm being serious! I'm
attuned to your distress cries. They come in on a certain
wavelength.' He wiggled his fingers at his head, miming a
frequency being received.

For a second, she actually considered that he might be
telling the truth. After all, she had no idea how alien
brains worked. But she knew he must be having her on
really. It wasn't as if she'd even been making any distress
cries.

She sniffed dismissively, and he grinned. 'I got bored
with the game,' he said. 'No challenge for a mind like
mine.'

'Did you beat Mickey's score?' she asked.

'What d'you think? Course I did. By several thousand

points, too. It might have been round about when I was doing the victory yell that he invited me to leave.'

Rose laughed incredulously. 'You let Mickey Smith chuck you out?'

The Doctor looked very slightly embarrassed. 'Told you, I'd had enough of the game,' he said. 'Come on, let's go and do something less boring instead.'

It was the least deserted part of the planet Toop, because it had two structures built on it. One resembled a giant pyramid that had had its top sliced off, like a boiled egg. But whereas a pyramid has only one entrance, this had hundreds. Sometimes, out of the corner of your eye, it might look as if the building was inside a dome, an immense upturned bowl made of faint purple lines. But there again, that might be a trick of the light.

The other building had no visible doors at all. It would be called big, although it was much smaller than the truncated pyramid, square and solid, constructed with little finesse.

Inside this building were many rooms, including what was known as the main control room. And inside the main control room, there was uproar. Quevvils were running back and forth, checking monitors and dials and read-outs. 'This is amazing!' squeaked one. 'This controller has mastered the game! The speed, the skill...'

'There is a long way to go yet,' said another, but his companions ignored the words of caution.

'The carrier has penetrated another barrier,' called a

third excitedly. 'Victory! Victory approaches!'

A stocky Quevvil started shooing a group of his glee-ful fellows into a series of booths. 'Ready yourselves! Do not delay! At the exact moment of success, you will be transported into the Mantodean stronghold – prepare yourselves for slaughter.'

The spiny backs of each Quevvil bristled as they read-ied themselves for action. One small Quevvil let a quill fly in excitement; it pinged off the back of the teleport booth and the stocky Quevvil who was in charge swung round at the sound. 'I... I'm sorry, Frinel,' the small Quevvil squeaked, terrified.

Frinel glowered. 'If it were not that I must ready myself for the moment of victory – the moment when I, with a single touch on this button, bring victory to us all... then you would be punished for your indiscipline.' His clawed finger was hovering over a huge red button, the control of the teleporter. 'Victory approaches...'

'Er... er... victory's stopped approaching,' said another Quevvil nervously, claw tapping a dial to make certain of the reading.

'The humans often pause for a while,' said another. 'They have no stamina. They are not warriors.'

A murmur of agreement passed throughout the room.

'No, the game's been shut off,' said the nervous Quevvil. 'We just have to hope that the carrier survives until the game is resumed...'

There was a groan from a Quevvil watching a monitor. 'Mantodeans in the sector...' he said. The others clustered around, even the Quevvils who had entered the teleport booths came out to see what was happening.

'It might not see the carrier…'

'No, two more coming round the corner… They've spotted it…'

'The one on the left's going to get it… Stupid carrier, just standing there…'

'It can't do anything else without a controller…'

'And there it goes. Hook up another carrier, back at the beginning, for when the controller returns…'

The leader, Frinel, grunted. 'I want that controller. No other has shown such skill! This is the controller who will bring us to our destiny at last! Track the signal. Send a message to our Earth agents. He will play the game for us – under our control.' He paused. 'And talking of control…'

He lumbered round, till his back was facing the rest. Then with a swish, he sent a barrage of quills flying towards the hapless small Quevvil from the teleport booth. The Quevvil collapsed to the floor.

'Discipline must be maintained,' said Frinel.

Mickey Smith was beginning to regret throwing out the Doctor, not because he wanted the smug git's company, but because it was obvious that Rose wasn't coming back with the milk and biscuits now her older man had left. He began an expedition through the kitchen cupboards, but there was nothing much except an old box of cereal and a giant jar of pickled onions that had been a recent present from Rose's mum. He unscrewed the lid, selected an onion and began to crunch thoughtfully.

So the Doctor was taller than him, and better-looking than him, and had saved the world more times than he had. He could cope with all that. But it was a bit much when the bloke even thrashed him at video games, because that was an Earth thing, a Mickey thing, and he should be allowed to win out there at least.

It was just because it was this new, weirdo game. *Grand Theft Auto*, or *Gran Turismo*, or even Sonic the bleedin' Hedgehog, and the Doctor wouldn't have stood a chance. But this game, with its jerky viewpoint and freaky graphics – it took time to get used to. Mickey hadn't played it nearly enough yet. Taking another onion, Mickey sauntered back into the other room and switched the games console back on. He was going to master this thing, and then next time the Doctor turned up on his doorstep he'd challenge him to a game – just a little game, Doctor, not scared I'll beat you, are you, Doctor? – and then he'd show the time-travelling show-off…

But the console was playing up. There were all these lights flashing and it was making this high-pitched sound, and there was no picture on the screen at all.

And then Mickey's front door crashed open.

For a second, when he saw Percy Porcupine standing in the doorway, Mickey had the mad idea that they knew his console had gone wrong and had sent someone round to sort it. But he knew that was stupid. That wasn't how things worked. And the bloke – or girl, who knew which was inside the costume? – hadn't even knocked on the door.

And then, because he remembered the sort of things that happened when the Doctor was about, he suddenly realised that this wasn't a bloke – or a girl – in a costume after all. So when the porcupine pointed a gun at him, he really wasn't surprised at all.

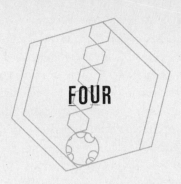

FOUR

Robert had always suspected that his mum wasn't his real mum. And he knew, knew with a passionate certainty, that deep inside he was different. Special. Not like other boys.

Then one day, the proof had come. The letter. The wonderful, glorious letter. 'Dear Mr Watson, We beg to inform you that you are really a wizard. We will expect you at Dozbin's Magical College at the beginning of next term.'

And his mum had had to admit that he wasn't really her son. His parents had been famous sorcerers, possibly the most brilliant sorcerers there had ever been, but they'd been killed by an evil wizard. It was suspected that the evil wizard had been trying to kill Robert, because he was going to be the most powerful wizard that had ever lived. So Robert had been smuggled away as a baby, and given to the most pathetic, feeble, stupid, rubbishy woman they could find, so no one would suspect.

But now the evil wizard was threatening to take over the world, and Robert had to go to Magical College to learn spells so he could defeat him once and for all, and all the kids who had ever teased

Robert would look at him in awe and the girls would love him...

He had to pack his suitcase to go to Magical College.

He was packing his suitcase to go to *Magical College*.

Not to go on holiday, he didn't want to go on holiday, 'a holiday in the sun, Bobbles, oh, we'll have a wonderful time,' but it wasn't the sun part or the holiday part that bothered him, it was the Mum part. He could be quite happy lying on a beach, sunglasses hopefully hiding the fact that he was watching the girls in their bikinis – dreaming that any minute now they'd look back at him, and it wouldn't be with pity or disdain for the skinny kid with pale skin and spots, it'd be with understanding as they divined that his soul was the twin of theirs, and it made them want him, need him, be desperate for him...

But he had his mum with him.

His mum who called him 'Bobbles', even in front of his friends, even in front of girls. His mum, who'd suddenly start rubbing sun-tan lotion on his back while he was chilling on the sand, like he was six years old.

Who read out things from her horrible women's magazines really loudly, so everyone could hear and know that she liked really rubbish things.

Who wore rubbish clothes and rubbish shoes and really hideous sunglasses just to embarrass him.

Who'd tell complete strangers about all the 'funny little things' he'd ever done, from bed-wetting onwards.

Who'd make a fuss in restaurants by actually asking questions about the food, making him want to bury his head in shame.

Mum hadn't thought they'd be able to afford a holiday this year, and he was so glad, because he could stay in his room all summer and listen to CDs and read books and think about how when he went down the shops he might bump into Suzie Price and they'd get talking and she'd hint that she thought he was a really great guy; which was much better than really going down the shops, because he might really bump into Suzie Price and none of the rest of it would happen, which would spoil the daydream completely.

And his mum, who did go down the shops, had won him this games thing, which only had one game with it but was really good anyway and he'd been playing it loads and was going to win the prize and he was quite happy to keep on doing that for the summer.

But then she'd won this holiday. And it didn't say anywhere on the card if it was for one person or the whole family, but Mum said that these things were always for families so she was sure it would be OK. And he prayed that it wouldn't be, that it'd be just for her, and she'd go off without him and miraculously decide he was old enough to be left on his own and he could be happy. But she'd asked, and said she wouldn't go if she couldn't take her Bobbles, and they'd said it was fine.

So he was packing his suitcase to go on holiday.

...and when he arrived at Magical College, the head sorcerer shook him by the hand and said, 'Robert Watson! This is such an honour. I know you're going to be naturally talented at absolutely everything. Because you're special.'

* * *

'Or we could go back to your mum's, if you want,' said the Doctor, and Rose couldn't help thinking he sounded unenthusiastic.

'I told her we'd be back for tea,' she said. 'We could do something until then. I know there's not time to save the whole world, but if we can find something smaller that needs saving, like a village or something, we could probably manage that.'

'So saving you from a knife-wielding thug doesn't count as my good deed for the day?' he asked.

'Yeah, I never got that,' said Rose. 'How Scouts and Brownies and stuff only had to do one good deed a day. I mean, if they, I don't know, saw someone drowning, but they'd already helped an old lady across the road, would they let them sink?'

The Doctor grinned. 'Yeah, the Scout law's really strict on that sort of thing. "You will do exactly one good deed a day and no more." If they accidentally did an extra good deed, they'd have to go and kick a puppy or something to balance it out, or they wouldn't be allowed to go camping.'

She thought for a moment. 'Did you have stuff like that?' she asked, genuinely curious. 'Space Scouts, or something.'

He nodded. 'Oh yeah. I got merit badges in time travel, monstrithology, interfering in the destinies of planets and cookery.'

'Monstrithology?'

The Doctor grinned. 'Monster spotting. Or, I might've just made it up.'

They carried on down the road. There were all these

posters, all along the street, all these giant porcupines wanting you to buy stuff and get free prizes.

'It looks so cheap,' said Rose. 'They've not even got proper posters done, it's just photos of people dressed up as porcupines.'

The Doctor walked up to a poster on the side of a phone box, so his nose was inches away. He was staring at it hard.

'If you're wondering why we still have phone boxes when everyone's got mobiles these days, I don't know,' Rose said. She reached into her pocket, to make the point. Her phone wasn't there.

'It's probably for daft people who leave their phones at their mum's,' said the Doctor, still staring at the poster. 'Come on, we're going into town.'

'Why?'

'Monstrithology. I want to find out how it's possible for a human to fit inside a costume like that. See the wrists? And the knees? I'd have said it couldn't be done.'

Rose almost jumped into the air. 'So it's aliens? Aliens taking over the planet via shopping?'

The Doctor shrugged. 'Don't have to be trying to take over the planet, just cos they're aliens. I'm not trying to take over the planet. The Cookie Monster isn't trying to take over the planet. Well, not the bits which don't involve cookies.'

She gave him a look. 'Cookie Monster is a puppet.'

He just smiled knowingly.

'He's got someone's hand up him and some bloke does his voice!'

The Doctor smiled again. 'You humans are so gullible.'

'You mean he's really an alien? Cookie Monster?'

Now the Doctor laughed. 'You humans are *so* gullible!'

A bus was drawing up to the kerb just ahead. The Doctor grabbed Rose's hand and they ran for it, leaping on just as it was pulling away again. The driver glared at them, especially when he found out the Doctor actually wanted to pay money for a ticket. He didn't notice that the travel card Rose waved at him had run out a year before.

'I'm such a criminal,' she said, swinging into a seat.

'Yeah, well, don't expect me to pay your bail,' the Doctor replied.

'So, are they really aliens?' she whispered, leaning in close so the nosy old biddies in the seat in front couldn't hear. They'd given Rose and the Doctor disapproving looks as they'd jumped on board; Rose wasn't sure if it was because the bus had already been moving or because they thought the Doctor was 'old enough to be her father' and didn't think much of that. Probably the latter. She felt like shouting at them, 'So, how d'you know he's *not* my father then?'

'I don't know,' he answered. 'Might be. Probably just a dodgy picture, Photoshop or something.'

'Oh,' she said. 'That seems like cheating, somehow. Anyway, where are we going?'

'Bit of shopping, bit of monster spotting…'

'Just in case?'

'Just in case.'

The Percy Porcupine booth was right slap bang in the middle of the high street, covered in posters. 'I wonder if aliens bother with getting planning permission,' said Rose. 'That could be a clue.'

There was a little queue outside the booth, a couple of people, tickets in hand. The Doctor and Rose joined the line, and watched the winners hold up their tickets to a little panel with a red light on it. The light went green as the first person was bleeped into the booth, and the door slid closed behind them. The light turned red again.

'Pretty elaborate security for a lottery thing,' Rose said. 'Or maybe they just don't want people stealing the prizes. Or they're expecting the games consoles to break down and don't want to have to deal with a load of irate computer geeks.'

'Anyway, looks like you need a winning card to get in,' said the Doctor. 'It's like *Charlie and the Chocolate Factory* all over again.'

The first man came out, a boxed-up games console in hand. The door slid back decisively behind him. The second queuer, a woman, held up her ticket. The Doctor and Rose sidled close, and the woman frowned. 'Excuse us,' said the Doctor, giving her a charming smile, 'we just wanna…'

But she'd nipped through the opening door, and it slammed shut behind her before the Doctor could even get a foot in the gap.

'We'll just wait here till she comes out,' said the Doctor, poised ready to dive in.

'And how are you going to explain this if they aren't aliens?' asked Rose.

'Won't have committed any crime,' he said. 'I'll say I've

got stuck on level six of *Death to Mantodeans* and I'm desperate for some gaming hints.'

Something caught Rose's attention out of the corner of her eye. 'Hey, isn't that the woman who just went in?' she said.

The Doctor looked up. 'Yes!' he said, staring at the woman, who was walking away from them, carrying a box. 'I think it is.'

Rose was thinking hard. 'Then this proves it!' she said. 'They must be aliens. They're luring people into these little huts, then they're duplicating them, robots or something. That's why they're so security conscious! They don't want us to see the machinery!'

'Or,' said the Doctor, who had wandered round the other side of the booth and was beckoning to her, 'they were worried we were trying to sneak in, so sent her out the back door.'

He took his sonic screwdriver from his pocket. 'Let's see what their defences are made of,' he said.

Rose was darting anxious glances up and down the street. 'We are being a bit obvious here,' she said. 'Couldn't we just try to win something instead?'

The Doctor was holding the sonic screwdriver in front of the little panel. The screwdriver was buzzing away, but the light remained obstinately red.

'Oh, all right,' he said, putting it back in his leather jacket. 'This doesn't seem to want to open. Which hints at alien involvement, yeah,' he added to her unspoken question.

It was easy to find a shop that carried the promotion;

it'd have been harder to find one that didn't. The Doctor bought a toothbrush. Rose bought a bar of chocolate. They rejoined forces to compare scratchcards.

"'Sorry, you've not won this time! Please try again!'" she said.

'Yeah, me too,' said the Doctor, taking the losing card from her and putting both of them in a coat pocket. 'Shall we try again?'

'OK,' she said. 'But can we go into another shop? It's embarrassing if we keep buying bits. Everyone'll know we just want to win something.'

'Cos it'd be awful if we got a bit embarrassed while we were saving the world,' he said. 'Can put you right off doing good, that can.'

She accepted the criticism, but remained adamant. It was easier to do stuff like that on spaceships, or in the past, or whatever, because somehow you didn't mind what people thought of you as much. Like how on holiday you'd wear the sombrero and the novelty T-shirt that you'd never be seen dead in down the youth club. So they went to the shop next door. The Doctor bought a pad of Post-it notes. Rose bought a biro. *Sorry, you've not won this time! Please try again!*

In the next shop, Rose bought a can of drink. The Doctor, obviously tiring of the pursuit, rooted out a load of change and bought seventeen copies of the same newspaper, one at a time.

They stood outside the door, both scratching away at the silver covering on the cards, the Doctor occasionally handing out newspapers to passers-by. Not a single card was a winner, and they were running low on cash.

'I've got an idea,' said Rose suddenly. 'You know how these might be aliens, right?'

'Uh-huh.'

'So, their technology's going to be alien technology. If you got hold of one of those games consoles and took it apart…'

'Brilliant!' he said. 'It might give us an idea of what they're up to an' all.'

'Back to Mickey's then?'

He nodded. 'Yeah. You still got the teabags?'

She grinned. 'Yeah. Have we got enough money for another pint of milk, though?'

There was just enough left, so Rose popped back into the newsagent's. The man behind the counter handed her a scratchcard, which stupidly took her by surprise, because this was actually shopping they wanted. This is it, she thought. *Charlie and the Chocolate Factory*. When you're waiting, hoping, desperate to win, you never do. But then, out of the blue, you get another chance. And that's the one. That's how it works. She beamed to herself, imagining the Doctor's face when he saw her waving the winning card in triumph, and scratched off the silver with a fingernail.

Underneath, it read, 'Sorry, you've not won this time! Please try again!'

FIVE

The Doctor and Rose caught the bus back to the estate, and made their way to Mickey's flat. Rose didn't realise that something was wrong, not at first.

'Did you leave the door open when you left?' she said to the Doctor.

He shook his head, and he suddenly looked concerned. He went inside, peering here, there and everywhere. Rose followed him. The flat was empty. In the lounge, the games console lay on the table, and the telly was still switched on. On the floor was a half-eaten pickled onion, toothmarks clearly visible in it.

'Someone kicked in the door and caught him by surprise,' the Doctor said. He darted back outside the front door. 'Look at this,' he called. Rose followed him out, and he pushed the door to, pointing at scratches on its lower panel.

'Um…' she said.

'Claw marks,' he said. 'Whoever kicked open this door had clawed feet.'

'Like Percy the Porcupine?' she said.

'Exactly like Percy the Porcupine,' said the Doctor.

They went back inside the flat, the Doctor closing the door behind them. 'Amazed his telly's still here, if the door's been open long,' he said.

'Hey,' said Rose, offended. 'You don't live here. You're not allowed to say things like that.'

'Is that how it works then?'

She nodded, sitting down on a chair and surveying the room for clues. 'Yeah. Like how I'd have a go at anyone who called you a cocky know-it-all who never listens to a word I say, but I'm...'

She broke off. The Doctor wasn't listening to her. He'd picked up the abandoned games console, and was prising off the back. He started poking around inside. 'Definitely alien,' he said. 'Bother.'

'Not just really advanced human?'

He shook his head. 'Nope.'

'D'you reckon they've gone around kidnapping anyone who's got one?'

He shook his head. 'There must be loads of the things out there. I think someone would've noticed. And what would be the point of that? No, they've taken Mickey for a reason. And I'd say it was fairly obvious what that reason was.'

Rose thought for a moment, leaning forward in concentration. 'For you, maybe, alien big-brain... It's gotta be something to do with this game... But Mickey'd been playing it for a bit with nothing happening...' She suddenly thumped the arm of the chair as realisation struck. 'And then you came along, and beat his score, and if I know you, probably the scores of everyone else who's ever played it in, like, two minutes. And they're monitoring the scores somehow so they send out troops to find this genius and carry him off. But they got Mickey instead. Right?'

The Doctor was now putting the games console back together. 'You get there in the end,' he said, giving her a grin. 'You'd have thought the moment they saw the lack of intelligence in his eyes they'd have realised he wasn't the one they wanted, though.'

Rose frowned. 'Like I was saying, you don't get to say stuff like that. Anyway, he's not thick. He's got GCSEs.'

'I apologise,' said the Doctor, smiling, not looking sorry in the slightest.

She decided to leave it. 'Well, anyway, what do they want with him – with you? Has this all been some sort of bizarre alien intelligence test? Like they're looking for the most intelligent people and then they kidnap them to drain their brains?'

The Doctor opened his mouth to speak, and she almost shouted, 'Don't you say a word! You dare make a comment about Mickey's brain when it might be being sucked out by an alien right now!'

He'd shut his mouth at her yell, but opened it again now. 'Could be that. But it's a bit of a random way of going about it. I wouldn't worry. He's probably fine.'

She was almost comforted. 'Really?'

He looked sincere. 'Yeah. Really.' A pause. 'Well, probably. Tell you what, shall we go and rescue him?' He glanced at the LCD clock on the front of Mickey's video recorder. 'Still plenty of time before tea.'

She threw an 'I don't believe it' look at the ceiling. 'Well, yeah. I pretty much assumed we'd be going to rescue him.'

The Doctor plonked himself down on the other chair. 'All right then. I mean, I'm not saying I'll miss him now he's gone or anything. But I'd rather he didn't get kidnapped by aliens on my watch, you know?'

She nodded, biting back a remark. She still could never tell if he was pretending not to care, some dry humour sort of thing, or if he really didn't care. And on the whole, she thought it was probably better in the short term if she didn't find out one way or the other.

The Doctor didn't seem to be doing anything, though. She waited for a moment, and then said, 'Well? Thunderbirds are go, or what?'

'Or what,' he said. 'Or did you get a Brownie badge in porcupine tracking?'

She glared at him. 'It can't be that hard. Someone'll have noticed a giant porcupine walking about the place carrying someone in its arms, or whatever.'

The Doctor shook his head. 'Nah,' he said. 'Have a sniff.' She did so, and as she breathed in a sneeze took her by surprise.

'Ooh,' she said. 'Better make a wish.'

'How about, "I wish I knew where Mickey had been

teleported to"?' the Doctor suggested.

'Teleport?' she said. 'How can you tell?'

'Leaves a distinctive tingle in the air, teleportation,' the Doctor said. 'And means our porcupines are fairly technologically advanced an' all.'

She shivered, thinking of Mickey's atoms being broken down and zapped through the air. 'You've managed to reverse teleportation before,' she said, thinking back to one of their previous adventures.

'Yeah, if I was at the other end where the controls are,' he said. 'Sorry, no can do here. No, there's only one thing for it.' He grinned, and picked up the games console. 'Time to go fishing.'

It took her a moment, but she got it in the end. 'You're going to act as bait. You're going to play the game and hope they come and get you too.'

'Yup.' He pressed a button on the console. The legend 'Introduction' appeared on the screen, and the Doctor grimaced. 'Right back to the beginning.'

'At least you don't have to do the training level,' Rose said. 'Anyway, we might learn something.'

Dancing cartoon porcupines shimmied across the TV screen, eventually drawing back to reveal a grainy image of what Rose now knew to be the real aliens.

'Yeah, s'pose you're right,' said the Doctor, selecting an on-screen option.

A graphic flashed, and the introduction began.

There were a group of porcupine-aliens sitting round a table. It looked like a council of war.

'Fellow Quevvils,' said a porcupine who had salt-and-pepper facial hair and long quills curving back off his head like a deadly teddy boy, 'we meet to discuss the threat of the evil Mantodeans.' The picture cut to footage of the giant praying mantises, then back to the Quevvils at their table.

'But what can we do, Frinel?' said another of the aliens. 'We are at a stalemate! We cannot hurt the Mantodeans, and they cannot hurt us!'

Now it cut to a cartoon showing a Mantodean trying to fix its jaws round a Quevvil's thick, spiny neck, and finally giving up with a shrug of its feelers. Another cartoon showed a Quevvil shooting a barrage of quills at a Mantodean, only for them to bounce off the insectoid's tough exoskeleton.

'Looks as if nature had the right idea,' said the Doctor in an aside to Rose. 'Two species that could live together in harmony.' He snorted. 'Like that's ever going to happen anywhere in the universe.'

Back at the table, another Quevvil continued, 'We have tried to infiltrate the Mantodean stronghold.'

Cut to a structure rather like one of the great pyramids, only without the point. Mantodeans, dwarfed in comparison, scuttled in and out of the hundreds of doors around its base. The building seemed to be in the middle of a sandy nowhere.

'Looks like a desert planet,' said the Doctor to Rose. 'Porcupines and praying mantises are found in deserts on Earth. It'd make sense for creatures like that to have evolved there.'

'Really?' she said. 'Is that how the universe works?'

'Oh yeah,' he said.

'But the catacombs within are not fit for our impressive bulk,' continued the Quevvil, 'And the Mantodeans have seeded their stronghold with fiendish traps.'

The Quevvil called Frinel narrowed his watery pink eyes, showing his disdain for those who set fiendish traps. 'Which is why we turned to technology to defeat our foes, developing the extremely clever science of teleportation, to enable us to reach the very centre of the Mantodean stronghold, defeat the enemy, and incidentally provide access to the valuable mineral deposits below.'

'Aha,' said the Doctor. 'Look for the money, they always say.'

'But the dishonourable Mantodeans have turned to technology also,' said Frinel, snarling and showing stumpy but fearsome-looking yellow teeth.

'Porcupines are vegetarians, right?' said Rose, a bit nervously.

'They have protected their stronghold with a force field. It prevents teleportation! And worse, it is tuned in to Quevvil biology!'

A cartoon showed a Quevvil trying to run into the pyramid. With a sizzling sound and a lot of jagged lines, it was clearly fried.

'This is terrible!' cried one of the Quevvils at the council of war. 'What can we do?'

'I have had an idea,' said Frinel. 'We will scour the universe for aliens of great cunning and ingenuity. They will come to Toop and infiltrate the Mantodean stronghold for us. They will evade the traps, and get to the centre. And there they will place this.' He held up a shiny metal cube. 'This is the disruptor developed by our scientists. When placed within close range of the Mantodeans' computer banks it will disrupt all their technology, taking down the force field and allowing us to teleport in – to victory!'

'But where will we find such beings?' asked a Quevvil.

Another Quevvil came running up to the table. 'Frinel! Fellow Quevvils! I have found a planet within range of our teleporters, where the inhabitants are warlike and possessed of great guile.'

'And what is this planet?' said Frinel.

The screen cut to an image of a very familiar blue and green globe.

'It is… the Earth!' said the Quevvil.

'Now there's a turn-up for the books,' said the Doctor to Rose.

There was a whirring noise and a jump in the image, and suddenly they were with another Quevvil. A counter in the top right corner read '0'.

'Starting the game proper,' said the Doctor.

'Thank you for rising to the challenge, human,' said the Quevvil, holding out a disruptor. The Doctor pressed buttons, and the Quevvil took back its hands, now empty. In the bottom of the screen, a little icon appeared, labelled 'Disruptor: primed'. Then the Quevvil moved aside, revealing a window beyond which was a stretch of desert. In the distance was the enormous truncated pyramid of the Mantodean stronghold. 'The fate of our race is in your hands,' the Quevvil said, pulling a lever on the wall. The image shimmered, and suddenly they were looking at a completely different wall, containing a door. As the Doctor manipulated the controls, their point of view moved forward, towards the door.

'Nice when the villains present you with their whole plan in semi-animated form,' said the Doctor. 'Saves you having to be tied up and about to die before they'll reveal anything.'

'You really think they're telling the truth?' said Rose. 'About the force field, and why they need humans and everything?'

'Wouldn't be at all surprised.' The Doctor pressed a button, bringing the door into sharp relief. 'After all, no one's going to suspect it's true for a second. And even if they did, even if some human sat down to play this game and thought, "Hang on, maybe these are real aliens telling us about their real enemies," what are they gonna do about it? Try to tell anyone and they'd get locked up, trust me.'

'And I suppose no one on Earth would even care,' said Rose, thinking about it. 'What a bunch of aliens get up to on their own planet is hardly going to bother anyone.'

On the television, the first puzzle filled the screen. It was different to the mathematical one from last time the Doctor had played the game, but he solved it just as quickly. Once inside, he had to climb through vents, jump across chasms, and negotiate twisting and turning mazes.

'I can see why those fat porcupines couldn't manage this,' commented Rose, as the Doctor pressed a combination of buttons to navigate a series of long jumps on to tiny platforms. 'These are definitely meant for jumping insects.'

A couple of Mantodeans appeared at the end of a tunnel. The Doctor, leaning forward eagerly, pressed down hard on the controller's blue button. An icon appeared on the screen, a tiny pistol. 'Gun selected,' the graphics read. The Doctor's finger hovered over the red button.

Rose caught at his arm. 'You can't! You can't shoot them! They're real! You'd be killing them.'

The Doctor hurriedly pressed another button, and the Mantodeans snapped out of view as he ducked down a side tunnel. He sat back, looked at her. 'I was getting a bit carried away there.'

She gave him a half-smile. 'Yeah, me too. I mean, I wanted you to shoot them, for a second. Kill or be killed, and all that.'

He nodded. 'Only it isn't, you're right. Even if I have to start again, half an hour here or there probably won't make much difference to Mickey.'

She hadn't thought of that, and frowned. But although she'd have gunned down a dozen aliens to get to a Mickey being threatened in front of her, this was different. If the Doctor was right, he was just being made to play video games somewhere. Who knew, they might even be providing him with tea and biscuits. 'Have you got far to go, do you think?' she said. 'Before you get to the end of the game, I mean.'

'I'm not going to get to the end of the game,' he said, surprising her.

'What, is it too tricky?' She couldn't believe that was the case.

He laughed. 'As if!' Then he continued more seriously, 'We reckon I got further than any other player in a shorter time, right?'

'Right.' She nodded.

'And we reckon that's why they took Mickey. Probably because they thought he was their great hope, the only person likely to get to the end of the game. If what they're saying is true, they only need one person to get to the centre of this place, one person to activate their disruptor. Then that's it, game over. I do that, they'll have no need to come looking for me, they'll have achieved their purpose.' He gave her a meaningful look. 'And they'll have no need for Mickey any more, either.'

She understood, and shivered a little. 'Yeah, I get it.'

'So I'm just going to beat my previous score, and then I'm going to stop. And then they'll come and get me. And –' he broke off for a moment to jab at the controller – 'that's probably going to be any minute now.'

The Doctor's fingers flickered over the buttons, and then stopped. He gave a loud sigh, and placed the controller down on the table. 'There. One hundred points higher. Should get their attention.'

She felt like a bundle of nerves. Knowing a giant porcupine might appear out of thin air any second wasn't a relaxing thought. 'And what do we do when we get there?' she asked. 'What's the plan?'

'Ah,' he said. 'Probably should have checked you were up for it, really. You are up for it, aren't you? Dangerous, and all that.'

'Up for what?' He could be frustrating sometimes. 'But of course I am. You know I am. Always.'

He grinned. 'Yeah, I know that. Well, you'd better get behind this chair then.'

She glared at him. 'If you think I'm hiding while you run off into goodness knows what…'

'No, no, no,' he said hastily. 'Just, if they see both of us, they'll capture both of us, right? So they have to just see me, then there's one of us free to let the other out. Grab my ankle, then the teleportation field should take you as well. They won't be expecting someone else the other end. With any luck you'll be able to crawl away before they notice you.'

She was aghast. 'That's the brilliant plan?'

He held out his hands. 'It'll work! Those thick necks they've got, they won't be able to look down properly. You'll be way out of their field of vision.'

She wasn't convinced, but knew she probably couldn't come up with a better plan in time. 'Couldn't you be the one hiding?' she asked as a last resort.

'I'm over six foot!' he said. 'Catch me fitting behind this.' He patted the chair. 'And the shame of it! Hiding behind a chair from a monster? Me?'

Rose raised her eyebrows at him, but got up anyway, and crawled into the gap between the seat and the wall. The Doctor arranged a throw so it was more or less covering her. 'Oh, gross!' she called out. 'No one's hoovered back here since the Dark Ages.' A second later: 'I've just found a biscuit.' A second later: 'I've just found a pound coin.' A second later, worriedly: 'I don't know what I've just found, but I've put my elbow right in it…'

And a second later, she could smell something. A tang in the air, as if she'd just been spritzed with lemon juice. Her tongue and nostrils were fizzing.

'This is it,' said the Doctor, perching on the arm of the chair above her. 'Hold tight.'

She grabbed hold of his bony ankle, reflecting in a distracted way how odd it was that a 900-year-old alien from outer space wore diamond-print socks, just like they'd used to sell at the shop where she'd worked, £8.99 for three pairs, breathable cotton weave.

There was a crash; they'd smashed open the front door again. And then the Doctor was standing up, and saying really unconvincingly, 'Oh no! Why are you pointing a gun at me? I'll come quietly.'

And she just had time to see, from under the draped throw, a pair of clawed legs obscuring her view of the screen, which was showing a load of angry Mantodeans swarming around, clacking their jaws together.

'Game over,' Rose thought, and then everything disappeared.

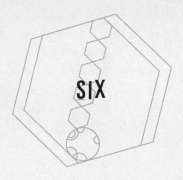

SIX

Rose was disorientated for a few seconds, and because of that she almost died. She felt sick and dizzy, and her skin tingled as if she'd just had a bath of Alka-Seltzer. She didn't think she'd ever be able to move again, or even know quite how bits of her body attached to other bits of her body ever again. But as her head began to clear she suddenly became aware that her arms were moving. She certainly hadn't consciously decided to move them, and she observed the strange phenomenon with detached interest for a few moments. Then the mental mists parted still further, and she realised that her arms were moving because she was clutching something with a death grip, and it was trying to shake her off. A moment later and she recognised it as an ankle, as the Doctor's ankle, and everything came flooding back. The Doctor was talking loudly, trying to distract attention from her. 'Where am I? What's all this about then?'

She unclenched her fingers, let go of the ankle. There

were other ankles in her line of vision, squat ankles covered in coarse black hair, leading to ugly clawed feet. A Quevvil's feet. Trying not to make a sound, not to move, she took in her surroundings. She was on a concrete floor, utterly exposed. But to one side was a litter of things: filing cabinets, chairs, a cracked computer monitor. She wriggled over to the pile as quickly and quietly as possible, began to slither behind it. Her legs were still sticking out when a door opened right next to her and she heard the *tink tink* of more claws on concrete. Lots more claws. Had she taken a fraction of a second longer to recover…

Not that she had recovered fully – she still felt nauseous and she found herself mentally checking herself, trying to work out if she'd been reassembled in exactly the right way. Had her fingers always been that long? Had her feet always been so small? She finally concluded that they had.

She wondered where they were. Still on Earth, she reckoned, thank goodness – she couldn't believe that any alien planet populated by giant porcupines would feature old computer chairs and doors with Chubb locks. And as Jackie had said, this was only a local promotion – well, let's hope they'd not ventured outside of London for their secret base, if that was where she was.

Through a gap in the junk, she could just see the protesting Doctor being bundled through a door on the other side of the room. She heard a yell of surprise in Mickey's voice before the door slammed shut, and felt a huge sense of relief. He was alive.

After a few minutes, the Quevvil who'd taken the Doctor into the room came out, alone. The key was turned in the lock. Rose mouthed a silent sigh of thanks – she'd been worried that they'd shut them in with some hideous alien lock, like the ones on the prize booth, and she'd never be able to let them out.

Mind you... how was she going to let them out anyway? There were four Quevvils in the room with her, and there was no way she could get over to the door without them seeing her, however low on the ground she kept. She'd just have to hope they left. But they were gazing at a couple of monitor screens, seemingly transfixed. On the screens, she could see complex 3D graphics. She suspected they were plans of this Mantodean stronghold they wanted infiltrated, and perhaps were representing the gaming progress of the Doctor and Mickey. But she couldn't see *how* exactly – it made no sense to her.

She waited, and waited, trying to gently flex her muscles so her legs didn't go to sleep in case she had to make a quick getaway. If it came to it, there was always the other door, the one the Quevvils had come through – she hadn't heard a key turn in the lock.

The minutes crept slowly by. If only she had a way to distract them! But she just couldn't think of one, not one that'd keep them distracted for long enough, anyway. The Quevvils weren't even talking, she wasn't even learning stuff about the enemy, they were just staring at these screens. But then...

Something must have happened, something to do with

the game. All four of the Quevvils leaned forwards, muttering among themselves, pointing and commenting. Was this it? Was this enough of a distraction? No, it wasn't, there was still no way she could get to the locked door, but – but she could try for the other door.

The thought was barely in her mind before she'd acted; if she'd waited it might have been too late. She was on her feet, turning the handle, slipping out of the gap... She pulled the door to behind her and sprinted off, still silently, waiting for the shouts and the gunfire and the pursuit, any moment now, any moment...

But they didn't come. She'd made it!

She'd abandoned the Doctor and Mickey to their fates, but *she'd* made it...

No, that was being silly, this was all part of the plan. She couldn't distract the Quevvils while she was in the room, but she might find something out here. And at the very least, she'd have found an escape route for when she *did* get them out...

She looked around her. She was in a corridor lit with dim electric bulbs. There was another door, and there was a ladder leading up to a trapdoor in the ceiling.

She shinned up the ladder, but the trapdoor was protected with the dreaded hideous alien locks. Mentally crossing her fingers, she climbed back down and hurried over to the door at the far end. It was locked, but with an ordinary key. She turned it, still trying to be as quiet as possible, and slipped through. She took the key; locked the door behind her.

She almost sneezed as the must hit her nose. Piles of mouldy old newspapers and magazines tied up with string lined the walls; she left the door open for the light from the corridor and took a closer look, managing to discern, through the dust, 1970s copies of *Woman's Realm* ('knit a Rupert the Bear for a favourite grandchild') and the *Daily Telegraph* ('Nixon resigns'). Every step she made showed in the dust on the floor, and she felt like Neil Armstrong. Didn't they say that footsteps remained on the moon for ever, because there was no wind to disperse them? Perhaps one day the Doctor would take her there, and she could see for herself.

If they made it through this, that was.

On the other side of the room there were concrete steps, leading up to a door, with a thin sliver of light underneath. Daylight? She made her way up. The door was locked. She squinted through the keyhole, but couldn't see a thing. It had to be blocked by a key.

So... she could think of only one plan. It came solely from children's books, the adventures of the sort of young detectives who caught smugglers and jewel thieves, and she couldn't believe it would work in real life, but she had to give it a go.

She collected an aged, crackling *Woman's Realm*, and after a search discovered an ancient children's comic with its free gift of a lollipop still sellotaped to the cover. Trying not to think what damage the sweet would do to a child's insides after thirty years, she prised the sticky mess away from its long-term home, and climbed back up the steps. She shoved the magazine under the door, rammed the lolly stick into the lock, took a deep breath, crossed her fingers and *pushed*.

There was a dull thud on the other side. Trying not to get her hopes up too high, she pulled back the magazine.

And there, on top of a recipe for damson jam, was the key.

She was shaking as she put it in the lock. So close, so close... If they heard her now...

The door didn't want to open. It creaked like a door from a horror film. She expected the Quevvils to come running; she expected to find Dracula waiting for her on the other side.

But, to her amazement, she came out somewhere that she actually *knew*. It was the newsagent's shop where the Doctor had bought his seventeen *Guardians*; where she'd bought that last pint of milk, now in Mickey's fridge; where she'd totally failed to win on the scratchcards.

She considered briefly that the newsagent was in league with the aliens, but she couldn't see it somehow. He might be a bit grumpy, but he wasn't that bad. And the door into the shop obviously hadn't been opened for ages.

Luckily, no one seemed to have noticed her come in. The newsagent was serving a customer at the front of the shop, and he couldn't have heard the door opening over the loud background Radio One.

She slipped out of the front door, on to the street. There in front of her was the prize booth, the place that they'd totally failed to get into before. The Quevvils had obviously extended it down, linked it up with some of the old shop cellars. A nice little underground base that no one'd suspect.

But now what could she do?

She looked down the high street for inspiration. Woolworths. Chemist's. Chippie. She couldn't half fancy a portion of chips, swimming in salt and vinegar…

Something clicked, somewhere at the back of her mind. Something she'd once read, or seen on one of those *Wildlife on One* documentaries. Porcupines and salt. Porcupines would do anything for salt; they were like total salt addicts. Would it be too much to hope – yes, it would be, it would be far too much to hope that these creatures had the same craving, just because they looked like the Earth animal… But they *might* do, and it was the best plan she had…

She nipped into the chip shop. The smell was divine, but all she had was the pound coin she'd picked up from behind Mickey's chair; she couldn't afford to treat herself. But there was no one else in the shop, no one to create a distraction.

'Portion of chips, please,' she said. 'Wrapped.'

The pretty Chinese girl behind the counter slid a shovelful of golden-brown chips on to some paper. 'Salt and vinegar?' she asked.

'I'll do them myself,' said Rose, picking up the giant salt pot. 'Oh, and could I get a can of Coke?' She pointed to the fridge behind the counter, and the girl turned. And the instant she did, Rose was out of the door, salt cellar in hand, regretfully leaving the chips behind her. She waited for the girl to shout out, but it never came. Perhaps customers did runners all the time. It wasn't as if she'd nicked the chips. The girl might not have noticed the absence of the salt. It was the second time that day that Rose had been a minor criminal. But, after all, she was potentially saving the world.

Now came the next part of her plan, the part that relied totally on luck. Because if this bit didn't work, she might have to turn criminal for real, to get her hands on a winning scratchcard. But before that, she'd give it a go. She pulled the pound coin out of her jeans pocket, and strode back into the newsagent's.

'A hundred penny sweets, please,' she said.

Rose's fifty-eighth card was the lucky one. She was getting pretty fed up with scratching off the silver stuff only to find the inappropriately jolly message, 'Sorry, you've not won this time! Please try again!' She'd 'please try again'ed until she thought her fingernail was nearly worn down to the bone.

But here it was. Here was the winning card. She'd won a games console.

Rose hurried across to the prize booth. There was no queue. She placed her card in the slot, and after a few moments' delay the door opened up. She went in. Inside was a counter, and behind it was a Quevvil, its mouth twisted in what might have been meant to be a friendly smile. 'Congratulations!' it said. 'You have won! I will fetch your prize.'

It moved away from the counter, and Rose leaned over to look. There was a tiny room behind it, with another door at the back – and on the floor, a trapdoor. That was it! That must be the entrance to the corridor under the ground! Time for the final phase of her plan – if only it worked…

She stepped back from the counter, trying to keep as far away from it as possible. Then she removed the giant salt shaker, and sprinkled a tiny bit on the floor.

The reaction was almost instantaneous. It was much, much more than she'd hoped for. The Quevvil began sniffing. It raised its nose in the air like an ugly, spiny Bisto kid. Then it darted forwards, scrabbling over the counter, ungainly and desperate. As the creature sank to the floor, its black tongue darting out to lick up the treat, Rose followed its route in reverse, diving over the counter into the little room beyond. She tried the trapdoor, but it seemed locked from this side as well, and she didn't have time to experiment. So she upended the salt container, and scattered it all over the floor, making sure that some of it trickled down the sides of the trapdoor. And then she ran out of the far door, offering up thanks that the alien locks must only work from the outside, and she didn't have to make her way back past the maddened Quevvil scrabbling on the floor. She slammed the door behind her, and, ignoring the interested looks from passers-by, hurried back across to the newsagent's.

'Look, I've only got a limited number of them cards,' the newsagent said. 'If you're going to do that again, you can just buzz off somewhere else.'

Rose gave the man her most charming smile. 'Just browsing,' she said. She waited till he was once more distracted with a customer and then, praying he didn't have CCTV installed, nipped back through the door to the cellar.

She opened the door to the corridor and peered through the gap. Her plan was working! Boy, those giant porcupines must really love their salt. All four Quevvils were on the ground below the trapdoor, licking at the floor like thirsty puppies. As she watched, one of them got to its feet and started climbing awkwardly up the ladder, then the others followed. She couldn't see what the first one did to open the hatch, but open it he did. All four climbed through, and before it was shut again, she could hear an explosion of snuffling sounds from above, as the rest of the salt bounty was discovered.

The instant the trapdoor was shut, Rose moved. She gazed up as she reached it, but had no idea how to activate the alien lock. She gave the ladder a quick tug, but it was bolted too firmly to the wall. She had to keep the Quevvils at bay for as long as possible, though... She plunged her hands into her pockets, looking for inspiration. She couldn't afford to waste time... Only one thing occurred and she did it as quickly as possible, before hurrying into the first room, the one they'd teleported into. She locked the door behind her, not that it would keep out a determined Quevvil for long. Then she darted across to the other door, and turned the key. She opened the door, and there was the Doctor, and there was Mickey, tied to a couple of plastic chairs, playing the game.

'Surprise!' she called.

They both turned, enormous grins on their faces. 'What kept you?' said the Doctor.

SEVEN

Rose made as if to shut the door again, trapping the Doctor and Mickey in the Quevvils' basement once more. 'A bit of gratitude, please, or the rescue stops here and now,' she said, but she was grinning as broadly as they were.

'I take back everything I was saying about humans being useless,' said the Doctor.

'When were you saying that?' asked Rose, indignantly.

Mickey sighed. 'Oh, 'bout every other minute for the last hour.'

Rose glanced at her watch. It had taken her some time to effect the rescue. But better late than never. She moved over to them and began working on their bonds, Mickey first. Her instinct had been to release the Doctor first, and although that was just a perfectly natural choice, didn't mean a thing, somebody had to be first, she had an idea Mickey would take it more personally than that. And because she didn't want to admit that he would be right to do so, she'd changed her plan.

She looked at the Doctor, his elbows tied tightly to the chair arms so he had enough freedom to manipulate the control pad, but not enough to untie himself. 'Wish I had a camera,' she said. 'That'd be one for the album. Not to mention I could probably make a fortune from any alien bondage websites there are out there.'

'Does your mother know about your obsession with these "alien bondage websites"?' he replied.

'Why do you think she's so suspicious of you?' Rose said. 'I told her you were the mastermind behind them.'

'Are there really alien bondage websites?' asked Mickey.

Rose and the Doctor burst out laughing. 'Yeah, I'll give you the address when we get back,' said the Doctor.

'Don't be silly, I didn't really think there was…' Mickey continued hurriedly. Then, as the Doctor didn't stop laughing, he added, 'Although aliens being gagged, I can see the appeal of that.'

Rose finished untying Mickey, and turned her attention to the Doctor. Soon his ropes lay on the floor, and Rose waited for him to stand up so they could make their getaway. But he stayed sitting down, still holding the control pad.

'Hadn't we better be getting out of here?' she said urgently.

'Hang on a minute,' the Doctor said. 'I wanna try something. Sit down, Mickey.'

Mickey had stood up, eager to be getting going, but sat down at the Doctor's words, seemingly to his own surprise. 'But those things could be back any minute,' he said.

The Doctor shook his head, as if such things really didn't concern him. He gestured at the image on screen in front of him. 'Does any of this look familiar to you?'

Mickey looked at it. 'Nope.'

'Thought not. Can't have everyone doing the same thing at the same time.' The Doctor leaned across to look at Mickey's screen. 'And yours doesn't ring any bells with me. Except… look up there.'

Mickey obediently pressed the relevant buttons. There was a tunnel entrance visible in the top corner of the screen.

'I think I've seen that,' said the Doctor. 'Right back at the beginning. So if I can just reverse to that point…'

'You can remember every turn you made for an hour or so?' said Rose. 'Blimey. I get lost in Hampton Court maze.'

'Nah, that's easy,' said the Doctor dismissively. 'It's hardly even up to your shoulders.' He thought for a second. 'Mind you, it might've grown a bit since I was last there.'

'Yeah, well, I went in 1998 on a school trip,' said Rose. 'Every turn there were snogging couples taking advantage of being out of sight of the teachers. You're going to tell me you went in the 1700s or something, aren't you?'

He grinned. 'Not if you don't want me to. I'll tell you this, though, there were snogging couples using it even then. Had to be careful that their powdered wigs didn't get caught on twigs. Last thing you want, you lean in for a snog and suddenly this impressionable young lady's seeing your hairdo as nature intended. Puts you right off.'

'Don't tell me you know that from personal experience,' she said, glancing at the Doctor's closely cropped head and battered leather jacket and trying to imagine him in full Restoration get-up, velvet, brocade and periwig. 'I really don't want to know. Ewwww!'

The Doctor laughed, his eyes never leaving the screen. 'Not my scene,' he said.

As the minutes passed, Rose got increasingly nervous. 'I really reckon it'd be a good idea to get out of here,' she said. 'Those aliens are gonna be back here soon, and we don't have any weapons or nothing…'

'Just a bit longer…' said the Doctor, eyes fixed on the screen.

But Rose was feeling really agitated. 'Can't you do whatever you're doing back home, if we just got hold of a couple of consoles?'

He shook his head, although he said, 'Maybe. But if what I think is true, there's no time to lose…'

Rose suddenly remembered something. 'There's a sort of diagram out there,' she said, pointing through the door. 'Maybe that'd help you do it quicker.'

The Doctor darted through the door, and she heard him call, 'Yes!' He popped his head round the doorframe and gave her a thumbs-up. 'This'll do it!' he said. 'Rose, pick up the control pad, and do exactly what I tell you.'

'But I don't do computer games!' she cried.

'You do now,' he replied.

So she sat there, and did her best to keep up with the rapid and complicated instructions the Doctor was calling through from the next room.

'Why's he doing this?' she asked Mickey.

'Dunno,' he said, shrugging. 'But it's been bugging him. He's been desperate to try this out. Trouble is, those Spiny Normans got a bit unhappy if you didn't stick with their plan, so he's not been able to do what he wanted.'

The Doctor's voice floated through again, sounding excited: 'This is it, any minute now... Keep an eye on your screens!'

Rose focused her gaze in front of her. But suddenly the control pad in her hand juddered. She tried pushing the button to carry on ahead, but it resisted her touch. It looked as if the same thing was happening to Mickey.

'Doctor!' she called out. 'It's going all funny!'

He hurried back in. 'Aha!' he said. 'That means we're getting close, I reckon. Got to maintain the fiction of the game, see. Thought there might be some sort of safeguards.' He took Rose's control pad and prised off the cover, then began poking around inside it with his sonic screwdriver. Having put the cover back on, he handed it to her. 'There,' he said. 'See what that's like. Few adjustments and that plan out there, we should be able to get round this.'

She tried again, following the Doctor's continuing instructions. There was still a bit of resistance, but she could push through it now.

On the screen, the viewpoint was jogging forward, jiggling up and down as if created by a camera held by a running man.

'Here we go!' called the Doctor.

And as Rose watched, something appeared on the screen, something she'd not seen in the game before. She glanced over at Mickey's screen. Something similar was coming into focus there too, coming closer and closer.

Both screens swam into focus at almost the same moment. Each screen showed... a figure. A human figure. A familiar human figure.

Mickey's screen showed a lad in his twenties. He had shoulder-length hair and was wearing glasses and a black T-shirt with a picture of screaming skulls on it.

Rose's screen showed a woman in her sixties, wearing a tea-cosy hat and a buttoned-up coat. Both had flashing discs sticking to their foreheads. Both had metal cubes – the disruptor of the game's introduction – strapped round their necks.

'I've seen him down the pub,' said Mickey, sounding confused.

'That's Mrs Hall,' said Rose, feeling a bit shell-shocked. 'Mum said she'd gone on holiday.'

The Doctor had come back into the room. He crouched down next to Rose. 'Your mum said she'd won a holiday. On the scratchcards.' He waited for that to sink in.

Rose turned to stare at him. 'There are real people playing the games?' she said, making sure it was a question, giving him the opportunity to tell her, no, don't be stupid, Rose, what a ridiculous idea…

'Yes,' he said, his jaw set in anger. 'Here you go, humans, have something for nothing. Oh, wait, actually we want something in return after all. You think you're getting a holiday, well, let's make it an action-packed one. Come to our planet and die for us.'

Rose felt sick. 'All those people – all those people who've won holidays…' She looked at the screens again. Mrs Hall was staring, her eyes trying to say something to the lad from the pub. The lad from the pub was looking the same, desperate and scared.

Mickey dropped his control pad, his eyes wide with horror. 'What happens when you lose the game?' he yelled. 'What happens? What happens when you see those insects coming towards you and they open their jaws? What happens when it says "game over"?'

Rose turned back to the Doctor, hoping for… She didn't really know what she was hoping for. For him to put it right, she guessed. To wave a magic wand and make it OK again, or better yet, to make it never have happened at all. 'Did you know?' she said, trying not to sound as if she was accusing him. 'Did you know what was happening?'

He shook his head. 'I didn't, no. I just thought there was something going on. Once we knew it was happening for real, I wanted to see what they were using to play the games.'

Mickey suddenly pointed a trembling finger at the screen in front of him. 'Oh no, oh no, oh no,' he muttered. As Rose looked, the green forelimb of a Mantodean appeared, waving at the side of the screen.

'Don't just sit there!' shouted the Doctor. 'Get them out of there!'

Rose pressed a button. On Mickey's screen, she saw the black T-shirt bloke turn to his right. Her hands were shaking. 'I can't do this!' she said. 'I can't control a person like they're a toy!'

The Doctor grabbed the controller from her. He started manipulating the controls, and in seconds the lad had disappeared from Mickey's screen, but the Mantodean was still there. Mickey had dived for the controller that he'd dropped on the floor, but he wasn't quick enough. He began to stab frantically, desperately, at the buttons, trying to move Mrs Hall – to reach for the gun – anything...

The mandibles of the Mantodean filled the screen.

And then there was just the simple phrase: 'Game over'.

'Sorry, you've not won this time,' whispered Rose, numbly. 'Please try again.'

Mickey leaned over the side of his chair and began to heave. Rose put out a hand to touch his arm, to comfort him, but he shrugged it off. 'I killed her,' he said. 'I just killed someone.'

The Doctor was still at the controls, eyes glued to the screen, face tense with concentration. 'Come on, come on,' he was murmuring. 'Not far now, nearly out...'

Rose was still feeling nauseous, but then something happened to make her stomach churn even more. She heard a noise. It sounded as if the trapdoor was being opened. 'Quick! Quick!' she yelled, panic hitting her.

'Nearly out!' called the Doctor. 'Here we go… There's the exit…'

The three of them stared at the Doctor's screen, adrenalin pumping.

'You're gonna make it!' said Mickey. 'Come on, come on…'

The exit was getting closer and closer. Rose imagined the lad, sweat running off his forehead, legs pumping as the Doctor propelled him towards freedom. Five more steps… four more steps, three, two…

'You're there!' said Mickey. 'Come on!'

Sand filled the screen, the landscape outside the pyramid, one more step and he'd be out…

With a press of a button, the Doctor helped the black T-shirted lad, the bloke Mickey had seen down the pub, take the final step to freedom.

And the screen went white, blinding white.

They gazed in disbelief as the light faded and the legend appeared: 'Game over'.

The Doctor threw the control pad on the floor. 'No!' he yelled. 'No, no, no!'

'What happened?' asked Mickey, still looking at the screen.

'They must've booby-trapped him or something. Something to stop people leaving once they're in there. Try to escape, and you get blown up.'

Rose hadn't quite taken this in when she heard the

noise again. 'The Quevvils are coming!' she said. 'We've gotta get away from here!'

They raced out into the first room. The door to the corridor was still locked. Rose put an ear to it. 'I don't think they're down yet,' she said. 'Shall we make a run for it?'

But the Doctor had found something, some sort of receptor built into the wall. 'I think I can reverse the tele-portation field,' he said. 'Send you back to Mickey's flat.' He waved his sonic screwdriver at her.

'Think you can, or know you can?' said Rose. 'I'd rather take my chances with an angry porcupine than end up with my atoms scattered to the four winds.' And then she took in the rest of what he'd said. 'What do you mean, send us back? What about you?'

He frowned, but didn't stop what he was doing. 'One, I'll probably have to stay here to operate this. Two, I need to find out stuff. Like, where their planet is.'

'So we can go there and rescue everyone?' said Rose.

'Something like that,' said the Doctor, twisting the end of his sonic screwdriver so it emitted a high-pitched hum. 'Just need a few more minutes here... D'you reckon those Quevvils are down yet?'

There was a loud thud from outside the door. 'Sounds like one just fell off the ladder,' said Mickey.

Rose smiled for the first time in quite a few minutes. 'I lip-balmed the rungs,' she said, producing from her pocket a pot that now contained only faint traces of cherry-scented gunk. 'Thought it might slow them down.'

The Doctor was now tapping on a keypad. 'Here we go,' he said. 'You two, come here.'

Rose and Mickey walked over to where he indicated. They were standing right in the middle of the room. The Doctor put his hands on Rose's shoulders, and looked deep into her eyes, that look that made her know she'd do whatever he was going to ask of her, however dangerous it was. 'I want you to collect up the games,' he said. 'As many as you can. We've got to stop people playing it. At the moment it's the only way we might be able to prevent more deaths.

'All right,' she said. 'But people aren't going to just hand them over – they'll think I'm trying to steal them or something.'

There was a sound from outside the door.

'You'll think of something,' said the Doctor, hurriedly. 'Right, off you go. I'll see you later. Meet you at your mum's.'

Rose smiled an acknowledgement.

The Doctor raised his hand to operate the controls.

The door burst open.

The Quevvil raised its gun.

The Doctor's hand came down.

Everything went fuzzy again.

Rose wanted to throw up. It was just as bad the second time. But her vision slowly cleared. She found she was face-down on carpet, but it was familiar carpet. The Doctor had done it! They were back in Mickey's living room, right on the very spot from which she'd vanished earlier. 'We made it!' she groaned, climbing to her knees.

There was no answer. 'Mickey?' she said. Feebly, she shuffled round to the front of the chair. Mickey had also materialised face-down on the floor, but he'd made no effort to move. 'Come on, you lazy lump,' said Rose, trying to jolly him along. 'If I can get up, you can.' But Mickey still didn't move. 'Mickey?' she said again, suddenly scared. She reached out with a hand. He didn't stir. She used both hands, managed to roll him over.

Then she realised. The Quevvil had managed to fire its gun before they had been zapped away. And it had hit Mickey.

EIGHT

There's a war on, Robert, and you're our only hope. You are the Chosen One, the one boy in all the world. You must fight the forces of darkness.

And by the way, your mum? She's not your real mum. How could the Chosen One have a mum like that? You must go to this ordinary coach station

only it doesn't look like a coach station, it looks like a fortress

where you will be transported to your destiny

here we are, this is the collection point, this is where we were supposed to go, now aren't you looking forward to it?

But it was really weird because the stupid promotional people were still wearing their costumes. And then they'd been taken into this strange room, and they'd been zapped to his destiny.

To an alien planet.

And it was real.

These are aliens, they are called Quevvils and they

look a bit like porcupines, and they are in a war against these giant insects called the Mantodeans. They've been at war a long time, and they've developed all sorts of technology, but the Mantodeans have this force field round their stronghold which kills Quevvils and stops teleportation, and so they need humans to get through it, *and you are the one boy in all the world who can save their race… This scratchcard promotion was all just a clever plan to get you here, to bring you to our rescue – we arranged for your mum (not that she is your mum) to win a holiday in the sun so you could embrace your destiny…*

They hadn't even totally lied, not really. There was sun and there was sand, just like they'd said, because this planet was desert stretching out for as far as you could see.

But it wasn't a holiday.

They'd grabbed people one by one, and stuck these things on their heads. Into their heads.

'All carriers augmented, Frinel.'

'Place them in the holding pen. The controller that will bring us victory has been located on Earth. Carriers must be prepared.' *All except the boy Robert, he is the chosen one – he is the one who will bring us victory…*

'Bobbles, darling, it'll be all right, Bobbles, it'll be all right…'

It wasn't fair. He was really scared, and this was terrible and real, and however much he'd longed for something out of the ordinary to happen this wasn't nice and it wasn't fun and it wasn't even the good scary that you got from being the hero because he wasn't the hero, he wasn't special and he wasn't important, he was just one of the nonentities and maybe there wasn't even a hero who'd turn up in time to rescue him and his mum.

And that really wasn't fair, because never, in any fantasy scenario in the world, did your mum get to go on the adventure too.

Rose stopped breathing for a second as she looked down at Mickey on the floor. Then she realised that he was still breathing, and so she allowed herself to do the same. But what damage had the Quevvil's gun done to him? At least with human guns, terrible as they were, you knew that a bullet went in one place and out another, but something like this – it could have scrambled his insides, for all Rose knew, and in rolling him over, she could have done any amount of damage. But just as she was wondering whether to attempt to move him into the recovery position, Mickey gave a groaning sigh and his hands fluttered by his sides. A second later, he opened his eyes, and gazed without focus towards the ceiling.

'Mickey?' Rose said urgently. 'Mickey, are you all right?'

He groaned again, and seemed to realise where he was. 'Ooph,' he said, exhaling heavily. Then a moment later, 'Ow!'

'Are you hurt?' asked Rose. 'Tell me where you hurt.'

Still groaning, Mickey propped himself up on his elbows. 'My leg! That bloomin' porcupine shot me in the leg!' he said indignantly.

Rose sighed in relief. 'Thank goodness for that.'

Mickey stared at her. 'Oh yeah, it's great. All hail to the porcupine for shooting Mickey in the leg.' He leaned forward and began to roll up his jeans leg. The skin on his right knee had exploded in blisters, and he winced sharply as the denim brushed against it.

'You know what I mean. All hail to the porcupine for not shooting Mickey somewhere where it might've been fatal.'

He appeared slightly mollified by that. 'Reckon they meant to, though. Probably just distracted by all of what was going on.'

'Probably dizzy with high blood pressure from a salt overdose,' said Rose.

'What about the Doctor, though? Reckon they got him?'

Rose had been trying not to think about that. 'Nah. He'd've got out of the way in time, easy. They were looking at us. And anyway, they want him to play that game. Even if they caught him, they wouldn't have hurt him.' But she wasn't anywhere near as sure as she sounded.

She helped Mickey up on to a chair. 'Will you be all right?' she said.

'Yeah, I'm fine, babe. I can always play a game to pass the time,' he said, and then added, 'I'm joking,' at her scandalised face. 'Of course I'm joking. Because one, it's obviously a joke. And two, someone's nicked the telly.'

Rose looked. He was right. 'Oh, what?!' she said. 'Oh, brilliant. He'll only go and say "I told you so" now.'

'Don't tell me, the Doctor,' said Mickey. 'I bet it's that

bloomin' Darren Pye that's nicked it. Anyway, that's not important now.'

Rose laughed. 'You, saying telly's not important?'

But Mickey suddenly looked as serious as she'd ever seen him. 'You just get out there and collect them up, all those consoles. You've gotta stop it, Rose. Stop them from killing people.' And then Mickey was trying to push himself up off the chair. 'I've gotta come with you, gotta help. Can't sit around when there are people still playing that game.' He started running on, babbling almost, panicking, about the people going on the holidays and the people sat at home, killing them... All very well for the Doctor to say it wasn't his fault, but Mickey still had the guilt, she could see that.

She tried to calm him down, explain why he couldn't help. 'You can hardly stand up, let alone get up and down all the stairs round here!' But looking at his agonised face, she had an idea. 'Tell you what, how about this? If we can get you to the computer, you can go online. Tell people not to play the game – that there's a fault or a bug, or it explodes if played for too long or something.'

'Yeah, all right,' he said. 'If the computer's still here.'

But Rose checked and it was, and so she helped him up, and he hobbled, leaning on her shoulder, into the bedroom.

They both heard it, the noise from outside. 'Front door's probably still open from where they kicked it in,' said Rose. 'Probably the wind blowing it.'

'Probably whoever nicked the telly come back for more,' said Mickey.

'Or only just left,' said Rose. 'Could have been out there the whole time…'

She went to look. Couldn't see anyone, but they'd have had plenty of time to get away. If there'd been anyone there at all.

She came back in, shut the door firmly behind her. Went back to Mickey, realised he was shaking. Shock.

She picked up the quilt from off the bed, wrapped it round him, went and made him hot, sweet tea, like they said you should. Looked in the cupboards in case there was brandy, even though she knew there'd just be beer. He was still shivering when she got back, but he was beginning to look embarrassed about it, so she knew he was getting a bit better.

They sat in silence for a while, neither knowing what to say. Then the silence was broken by the sound of a siren, somewhere on the estate outside, and it made her think of hospitals, of doctors. The other sort of doctor. But Mickey said he didn't need a doctor, and she couldn't force him. He kept saying she had to go, had to leave him and fetch those games, and she knew she must. 'You phone me if you need me,' she said, and then realised she didn't have her phone any more. So she said, 'I'll come back later. Let you know what's happening. Let you know when the Doctor's back.'

And she didn't allow herself to think *if* the Doctor gets back. Because she knew he'd be all right. He just had to be.

* * *

The Doctor was hiding behind the pile of old office equipment in the corner of the room. He'd dived into cover the moment he'd activated the teleporter, the moment the Quevvil had entered the room, and then he'd spent a sticky few seconds wondering if it'd spotted him or not. The Quevvil had fired an energy weapon, but he was pretty sure Rose and Mickey had vanished by then. Trouble was, they were dealing with split seconds here, and they were always tricky to judge. But he thought the two of them would be OK. Just hoped they'd do what he asked, collect up those games; reduce the number of players and you'd reduce the number of people being used, the number of people dying. He hoped.

He didn't have a particular plan, he just knew he had to find the location of the Quevvils' planet, so he could bring home all the people trapped there. And sort out the Quevvils as well, of course. They couldn't keep on doing this sort of thing. He'd known maniacs who played human chess – real chess, not symbolic – and that was bad enough, making a knight stick a lance through a castle, making a bishop decapitate a pawn. But there was something so prosaic about what the Quevvils were doing: just using humans to do their dirty work – or rather, worse, tricking humans into doing it. Using their greed. Playing on their desire to get a free lunch. And there ain't any such thing.

The other Quevvils had joined their fellow now, one of them limping a bit. Good ol' Rose and her lip balm. They seemed to be arguing about who would report the loss of the Doctor and Mickey to Frinel. The leader of the Quevvils was obviously feared.

'Frinel will be displeased!' a Quevvil said. 'We had assured him that victory was near at hand. He will have prepared for the final defeat of the Mantodeans.'

'Death to the Mantodeans!' shouted the other three Quevvils, shaking their fists in the air. Their arms were so short and stubby that, even at the fullest extent, they reached no higher than their snouts.

There was a beeping noise from the control panel in the wall. One of the Quevvils moved over to it. 'Incoming message,' he said. The Doctor pricked up his ears.

A voice came out of the panel, of a harsher timbre than those Quevvil voices the Doctor had heard so far. 'This is Frinel speaking. Respond, Earth party.'

The Quevvil said, 'Earth party here, Frinel. This is Revik.'

There was a snort from Frinel. 'Report status, Revik. You assured us you had found a controller who would complete the task. Two controllers, in fact. But the carrier controlled by one was killed by the Mantodeans. And the other was somehow allowed to remove his carrier from the Mantodean stronghold! Explain!'

Revik paused, obviously not relishing the task. 'We were forced to leave our positions temporarily,' he said at last. 'It was a matter of urgency. When we returned, it had happened as you describe it.'

'Then you will deal with the situation!' screeched Frinel through the speaker. 'Or you will be replaced!'

'It will be done as you say,' replied Revik.

A beep indicated that Frinel had terminated the link.

Revik turned back to the other Quevvils. 'We must recapture the controllers,' he said.

'But we do not know their location,' replied one of them. 'Unless they play the game again…'

'We do know their location,' said Revik. 'They obviously reversed the teleportation field. It will have returned them to their original location. We merely need to follow and retrieve them. Ready your weapons.'

Revik reached out a paw for the control panel. But the Doctor had already moved. Before the teleporter could be activated, he had grabbed hold of a cracked computer monitor, heaved it off the pile of junk, and thrown it as hard as he could. His aim was good. There was a shower of sparks as it smashed into the control panel. No one would be teleporting anywhere, certainly not to Mickey's flat. Rose and Mickey would be safe. On the other hand, though, dodgy vision or no, the Quevvils could now hardly fail to notice that there was someone else in the room with them.

The Doctor raised his hands above his head as he stood up straight. 'Hello,' he said. 'No need to go after anyone. You've got one of your controllers right here.'

Four guns were aimed straight at him.

'You don't want to shoot me,' he carried on. 'You were just running on to Frinel there how you were going to be getting me back. I've saved you the bother.'

One of the Quevvils turned to Revik. 'This is the

human who got the furthest with the task,' he said. 'He is the one most likely to bring us victory.'

'But he has destroyed our teleporter! We cannot return to Toop! He must be punished!' Revik's quills started to bristle. The Doctor couldn't decide which he'd prefer the least, being blasted with energy weapons or turned into a pincushion by an angry Revik.

'It is inconvenient. But it can be repaired,' said a Quevvil.

'And we must not return to Toop until a controller has completed the game,' said another Quevvil. 'This is the controller that will do it.'

All four seemed to agree. Revik relaxed, his quills no longer quivering. The guns, however, were not lowered.

'This controller shall play the game again,' he said. 'And this time, he will complete it. And we will watch him every second, no matter what – distractions – there are.'

The four guns gestured in the direction of the room with the games consoles, and the Doctor moved as indicated. Whatever happened, though, one thing was certain. He was not going to play the game again.

Rose decided to go to her own flat first. She could pick up her phone, and her mum'd probably know a few of the people who'd won stuff, that would be a start.

As she opened the door to the stairwell, she noticed a police car stopped out on the road. But as she looked, it started off again. Didn't have its lights on or anything, so probably wasn't important. Maybe it wasn't just Mickey who'd had a telly nicked. Hey, there was no sign of Darren Pye loitering around. Maybe he'd been in the back of it. Well, she could hope.

This time, Rose used her key. She pushed open the front door. 'Mum! You'll never believe it, there are only aliens here again… Mum?'

There was no reply. She pushed open the lounge door, but the telly was off and there was no sign of Jackie. She called down the hall, 'Mum? Are you home?' Still nothing. Oh, my god, they've got her too. The aliens have got her too!

No, that's silly. The front door was locked. She's fine.

Rose went into the kitchen. Empty. Mum's out, she thought. She's out, and she doesn't know there are aliens on the loose, but she's fine.

And then she saw the note. It was stuck on the fridge under a magnet that said 'Best Mum in the World', a Mother's Day present from years before. She sighed.

Dear Rose.

I won the holiday!!! Well, it wasn't me really, it was Dilys, she won two and she's given me one and said she'd only go if I did, you know what she's like about going abroad. Tried to ring but you'd left your phone here. Waited as long as I could but they said if we didn't go today we'd lose it, and Dilys really needs the break. Won't be for long, hope you're still here when I get back. Help yourself to anything. If you share a bedroom I don't want to know about it.

Love Mum xxx.

PS Took your phone, knew you wouldn't mind, so you can let me know what you're doing.

Rose wanted to scream. She tried to get angry, angry with her mum for being willing to rush off at a moment's notice, never mind that she'd got her daughter home for once, but her stomach had plummeted with fear and the anger couldn't drown it out, because she knew what these holidays were, what they really were, and she knew what might be happening to her mum right now. She thought she might be sick. 'You never get something for nothing!' she yelled, screwing up the note and throwing it across the room.

She took a deep breath, and then thought, the phone. I can phone her. I can let her know what's happening. They wouldn't have counted on that, on someone having a phone that works across space and time, couldn't possibly have counted on that. She'd phone her mum, tell her all about it, what was going on, and Jackie could lead a revolution and it'd all be OK until the Doctor could get there, wherever it was, and bring everyone back home.

And inside, a tiny voice was saying, but they'd know what was going on, they couldn't help noticing that they're not on an aeroplane going to Ibiza, they're being taken to an alien planet and made to fight and die, even knowing that no one's ever come back, so ringing up and going, 'Oh, you've been kidnapped by aliens,' isn't going to come as a big surprise and isn't going to help.

But, of course, she had to phone anyway.

It took her a second or two to remember her own number – you got out of the habit of giving it to people when you were trotting around the nineteenth century or whatever. But then she dialled.

It rang. And it rang and it rang and it rang.

She began to get panicky. The aliens would have heard the phone. They'd tracked it down, pounced on her mum. They'd think she was an alien because she had alien technology; they'd think she was a threat; they'd kill her.

Or maybe they'd heard the phone, and they were still tracking it down, and her mum was too scared to answer it but they hadn't found her yet, and if she left the phone ringing for just one more ring the aliens would find Jackie and kill her…

Or maybe if she left it for just one ring, Jackie would answer.

She left the phone ringing, knowing it was pointless, not being able to bring herself to put it down, to surrender that one chance of contact.

And then the phone said, 'The person you are calling has not responded. Please try again,' and there was a click and then the dial tone.

Slowly, reluctantly, Rose clicked off the handset.

NINE

All Rose could think of doing was, somehow, finding out where her mum had gone. Maybe she could win a holiday too, and follow her. She still had forty-two untouched scratchcards, after all. Perhaps one of them was a 'lucky' one.

Rose scrabbled in her pocket, dragged out the wodge of cards, began frantically scratching off the silvery covering. No. No. No. No. She began to despair of the Quevvils. Surely they wanted people to win? Surely they wanted an endless supply of players for their deadly games? So why couldn't they have stuck in a few more winning scratchcards?

Sixteen cards in, and she got a result: not a holiday but another games console. Which was no good, not what she wanted, but something. Twenty-one cards more, nearly at the end of the pile, and she got another one. Try to look on the bright side: at least that was two winning cards not in the hands of people who might use them, claim their consoles, kill some friends.

Not a single holiday in the whole lot. And Rose still didn't have a plan.

Maybe Jackie hadn't left the planet yet, maybe Rose could find out where the 'winners' were taken and go there. She'd think of a plan, she knew she would. For now, she decided, she had to get into town, as quickly as possible, and hope that by the time she got there she'd know what to do.

Rose left the flat, locking the door behind her, and hurried down to the road. She stuck out her arm as a bus approached, and it pulled into the kerb. She jumped on it, and waved her pass as she moved in the direction of a seat.

'Oi,' called the driver. 'Oi, you.'

After a second, Rose realised he was addressing her. She backtracked, and looked at him expectantly. 'Yes?'

'Let's see your pass again.'

Her heart sinking, she held it up, smiling, as if she knew that there wasn't really a problem.

'That's over a year out of date!'

She looked at it, so surprised. 'I'm really sorry. I must have picked up the wrong one by mistake. I won't do it again.'

But he wasn't to be swayed by a charming smile and an apologetic manner. 'That's £1.20, then.'

'I don't have any cash on me,' she said. Didn't say, I've got out of the habit; I haven't needed money for months.

'Can't let you on the bus then,' he said. By now the other passengers were starting to grumble. Holding everyone up. Young people these days. Thoughtless kids. Selfish cow.

'But it's really important,' she said. 'I've got to get to town. Please?'

'Not my problem,' said the driver, and she could tell that he was enjoying this, that it was the highlight of his day. 'I'm not moving this bus until you've got off it.'

'It's a matter of life or death!' she tried.

But the bus driver was implacable, and the noise from the other passengers was beginning to get ugly, and precious seconds were ticking away, so in the end she had to get off. What did they care that her mum could be on her way to an alien planet right now, could be on her way to her death? Even if she told them that, even if they believed her, they wouldn't care. The difference between life and death: one pound and twenty pee.

Hating them, hating humanity, Rose started half walking, half jogging her way into town.

After a bit of running around, a few shouts and threats and so on, the Doctor was leaning back in his chair, a gentleman of leisure. Eventually, faced with not many options, he'd voluntarily taken his old seat in the games room, hoping that the Quevvils would thus register him as being a prisoner again without remembering that prisoners are usually tied up. So far, it seemed to have worked. He was holding the control pad in his hands, but hadn't started playing the game again. If he had his way, that would never happen. He'd been trying to keep a conversation going instead, and had managed it for quite a while now, without, however, finding out anything of use.

'Bit of a waste,' he said to the Quevvil guarding him. 'Blowing up your pawns if they leave the game. Just means you've got to get more of 'em.'

'We cannot risk the carriers returning to our base,' said the Quevvil. 'If the primed disruptors were then activated… That is, in the game –'

The Doctor raised his eyebrows. 'Exactly how thick do you think I am? It's not a game, I have worked that out.'

The Quevvil seemed flustered. 'Humans do not have the intelligence…'

The Doctor didn't point out that he wasn't human. 'Yeah, you're right, teleport a couple of humans into your secret underground base, shoot ray guns at them, force them to play – they'll never work it out.'

The Quevvil snarled. 'Your mind cannot comprehend the truth.' It raised its gun. 'But you will play the game.'

'Don't think I will, thanks all the same,' said the Doctor. 'I'm a bit anti setting off to kill these Mantodeans who've done nothing to me. And I'm not that keen on risking the life of some poor kidnapped human, either.'

The Quevvil started to wave its gun – and then lowered it. It had a cunning look in its eyes that the Doctor didn't like.

'So far, you are the human who has progressed furthest into the Mantodean stronghold. But it is only a matter of time before others penetrate into the heart of it. We have waited for years; we can wait longer. We came to this planet and started in this small area to see if the idea had merit, if the humans were intelligent enough, if our technology was sufficient on Toop –' the Doctor grimaced in frustration; they kept merrily mentioning the name of their planet but it meant nothing to him, he'd never heard of it; why couldn't they drop its galactic co-ordinates into the conversation? – 'if it could cope with a small number of carriers and controllers. We hardly expected to find a controller who would succeed immediately – indeed, with hundreds of games out there, only a very few controllers have passed our training level, a mere handful showing themselves worthy of our dedicating our full resources to them. So we are already prepared to extend the plan. We will take it to more towns, across this country, and then to other countries. We will increase the number of winning cards. Humans are greedy: order them to aid us and they would protest, but make it seem like a prize, like something for only a select few… ha! They will snatch at any chance of getting something for nothing! The more humans who play the game, the more competent controllers we will find, and the more carriers we will need… If you played the game for us now and did as we wanted, got to the centre of the Mantodean stronghold, no more humans would have to die. But until someone succeeds, the game will continue to be played.'

'Stop calling it a game!' yelled the Doctor in fury. 'People are dying!'

'Our research suggested that death was a common pastime on Earth,' said the Quevvil. 'Humans spend much of their time killing. There is hardly a species on Earth that humans do not kill, including other humans. That, with your greed and cunning, was why you were considered ideal subjects for this task.'

'Yeah, we humans are a bit rubbish,' said the Doctor. 'A lot of us aren't very nice at all. I can't defend all that killing we do, all that greed and cunning. So I'm hardly going to sit here and commit genocide just to save a few of us, am I? What have these Mantodeans ever done to me?' He threw down the control pad, and slapped his forehead. 'Oh, hark at me, completely forgetting to mention I'm not human. You won't get a human to solve this "game" for you. Yeah, they're cunning and all that, they're pretty determined, and a few of them might even be geniuses like me. But not all that many. It's going to defeat them all in the end. You should sack your market researcher.'

The Quevvil didn't seem to know what to say to that. So it raised its gun again, and pointed it straight at the Doctor.

Rose arrived in town, but she still didn't have a plan. Get into the Quevvils' base, find the Doctor, hope he'd know what to do, how to save her mum? She hurried to the newsagent's shop. It was closed. She glanced at her watch: 5.40. The whole day had gone by without her noticing. She started to examine the lock, hastily pretending to be tying up her shoelace as a couple of uniformed policemen walked past, hoping they didn't notice that her shoes didn't have laces. But it was no good, she didn't have the faintest idea how to pick the lock, and the shop had a prominent alarm system. She'd be arrested before she got halfway to the cellar.

She turned her attention to the Quevvils' prize booth, a few metres away. Still didn't have a proper plan, but she couldn't just do nothing. Let's hope they're the sort of aliens who think all humans look alike. They barely saw me, she thought, trying to convince herself; just if they looked out when I was trying to get in with the Doctor, and there was only one of them when I was scattering salt all over the place, and they would have seen me only for a split second before we teleported away...

She'd have to risk it. She knew this wasn't the right plan, wasn't the one that would work, didn't have a hope, but it was all she could think of just now, and she'd have to risk them recognising her.

Rose went up to the booth, acting casual, nothing to indicate she knew these were aliens, nothing to say *you might have killed my mother.*

She got one of the winning cards out of her pocket, stuck it in the reader, waited to be allowed through the door. There was a Quevvil behind the counter. So much for her hope that the Quevvils couldn't tell humans apart – pot calling kettle, she had no idea if this was the one she'd encountered before or not.

The Quevvil produced a boxed games console and tried to hand it to her.

'I've already got one of those,' Rose said. 'I just wanted to ask a question. My mum's won one of your holidays and I need to get in touch with her urgently. Could you tell me if she's left yet?'

'I am sorry, that is not possible,' said the Quevvil, pushing forward the box.

'Is there a depot or something?' said Rose, her eyes darting all around the booth, hoping to discover some sort of clue.

'I am afraid I cannot give out that information,' said the Quevvil, still being insistent with the boxed game.

Rose lost it. 'Tell me what you've done with my mother!' she screamed. She grabbed the box, and threw it across the counter. It hit a pile of games, which collapsed with an almighty crash. The Quevvil's quills began to stand on end, and it suddenly hit Rose that this was an alien, an alien who didn't mind killing humans – it wasn't going to give her any information on Jackie, this was totally the wrong plan, and the door had closed behind her...

The Quevvil was holding the gun on the Doctor when a great noise came from above, as if something heavy had been dropped to the floor. The Quevvil glanced upwards, and the Doctor pounced. Pouncing on something covered in pointed quills possibly wasn't the most sensible move in the world, but the Quevvil was distracted as the Doctor managed to wrench its gun away, and in an instant he was out through the door. A barrage of spines soared through the air after him as he sprinted down the corridor, past the three Quevvils by the ladder to the trapdoor, presumably going to investigate the noise. He reached the far end of the corridor, and slammed the door behind him. A drumming noise told him that more quills were thudding into the heavy wood of the door. The key was on this side, and he turned it. It might keep them out for a while. He took a deep breath.

Rose had forgotten that the doors opened from the inside. She hit the control and dived out of the booth, praying that the Quevvil wouldn't follow her. It wouldn't, would it? Wouldn't want to make a fuss, make people think there was something odd going on, that they weren't what they said they were…

She stood by the booth, not knowing what to do next, panic threatening to overwhelm her. She wanted to throw more things.

Then a voice somewhere nearby said, 'Rose? Rose, sweetheart? Is everything all right?'

Of course everything wasn't all right, and it took Rose a few moments to calm down and pay attention to the tremulous voice. She finally turned round, to see an elderly lady wearing a pink plastic mac, a flowered head-scarf tied over her white permed curls. It didn't register initially. And then she realised, hardly daring to let herself hope. 'Dilys?' she said. 'But… but I thought you were going on this holiday with my mum…'

Dilys looked worried. 'I couldn't go on my own, Rose,

love. Since my Harold died, you know I don't like going places on my own, not even the bingo.' She held out a hand in which was a familiar piece of cardboard. 'I just came here to see if there was anything they could do about it, about your mum's. Shame she has to miss out.' She pushed the scratchcard towards Rose. 'Look, would you take this, Rose, dear? I feel so bad about what happened. I couldn't go now. Maybe your mum'll still want to, though, later. She can have this one, I know they said we had to go today, but you never know…'

Rose took the card, not really understanding what Dilys was saying, but the hope was growing, blossoming inside her. 'You mean my mum didn't go on the holiday either!'

But Dilys was still looking worried. 'You mean you don't know? They said they'd phone you, promised they'd let you know.'

The hope was being replaced by an ache, a heaviness in her stomach, and she blurted out, 'Tell me what, Dilys? Who was supposed to tell me what? Please, tell me!'

And poor Dilys, nervous and stuttering, began to tell her. 'I'm so sorry, Rose, love. I've got bad news…'

The Doctor had made it through the newsagent's cellar and into the shop without hearing any more from the Quevvils, save a few shouts and thuds. The newsagent had a big promotional Percy Porcupine poster on the wall, and the Doctor let out a few feelings by ripping it down and shredding it to bits. What the newsagent would think in the morning, he didn't really care. The door to the street was locked, but this presented few problems to someone who'd picked as many locks as the Doctor had. It was also alarmed, but the sonic screwdriver took care of that.

The street was fairly quiet when he stepped out of the shop – a few youths hanging around, drinking cheap lager out of cans; an occasional shop worker heading home. The booth where the Quevvils handed out their deadly prizes seemed deserted – whatever had caused the noise obviously long gone. The Doctor decided to leg it before they thought to pop out that way to pursue him. He ran off down the high street, heading back towards Rose's flat.

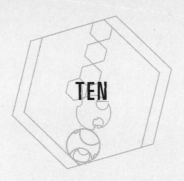

TEN

Rose looked at all the tubes and things leading into her mum, and felt sick again. Her mum was so protective of her, always had been. If Rose scraped her knee, Jackie'd be there to pick her up. She'd be down the school if anyone had had a go at Rose, have a word with whoever, not let Rose be left out or upset or picked on. It'd been embarrassing at times, but your mum protected you, that's what mums did.

But looking at her mum lying on the hospital trolley, black eye and purple cheek and dried blood under her nose, knowing that her mum was just a fragile human being, not a superhero, that was the worst feeling in the world.

And on top of that, now Rose was the one who was trying to save the world, and part of the world that had to be saved was her mum. That was so wrong.

Jackie's eyes flickered open. She smiled when she saw Rose. 'Oh, Christ, you're all right. My darling, you're all right.'

Rose stared. 'I'm fine. Don't worry about me.' Because why should her mum be worried about Rose, when she was in that state?

Jackie obviously saw that in her face. 'He said he was going to get you,' she said.

Rose leaned down, got closer to her. 'Who did? Mum, what happened to you? Was it the aliens? Did they find my phone? Did they think you were in league with the Doctor or something?'

Now it was Jackie's turn to stare. 'What are you going on about? It was that Neanderthal Darren Pye.'

Rose couldn't help herself, she almost felt a twinge of relief. Not aliens! Not her phone, not her fault!

But then she looked back at her mother, and the relief didn't last.

'They just told me you were in here, that you'd been hurt. What happened?'

Jackie looked reluctant. 'You'll only blame yourself…'

'Mum!' Now Rose really had to know.

'Oh, all right then.' Jackie propped herself up on the pillows. 'I was trying to find you. I'd called Mickey's but no one answered, but I thought I'd pop round, just on the off chance, on my way to meet Dilys. But I saw him. That Darren Pye. He was carrying a telly and I was willing to bet it wasn't his, and I might've said something. And he… he said… he said things about you. And I couldn't let him do that, so I gave him a piece of my mind.'

Rose closed her eyes, reluctantly picturing it, thinking of the sirens they'd heard, wondering if they'd been coming for her mum. If only she'd gone to investigate, if only…

'And he said that he owed you one for hitting him or something – you didn't hit him, did you, Rose, what d'you wanna go and do that for, asking for trouble? – and you were going to get it. But for now…' Jackie stumbled. 'For now, he'd make do with me.'

'Mum!'

'He just hit me a bit. Looks worse than it is.'

Rose knew that wasn't true. And she knew that for her mum to put a brave face on it, not ask for sympathy, well, it had to be pretty bad.

'Still, I got to jump the queue. There's hundreds out there in casualty, and I just got wheeled right in like a proper VIP, cubicle of my own, nurses running around cleaning and stitching and what-have-you.' She started to smile, but began coughing instead. Rose grabbed Jackie's hands and held on tight, trying not to cry, trying not to feel so helpless.

'Nicked everything I had, as well, that lout. Purse, keys, everything. Even my winning ticket,' she said, and Rose couldn't bring herself to tell her mum the truth about that winning ticket, not now, not while her mum looked so weak.

'Oh, and your phone too, love. Sorry. I'll get you a new one.' Jackie sighed. 'The police won't get it back, for all their "we'll do everything we can, Mrs Tyler". One was in just before you, said they'd been looking for him around the estate and he wasn't there. Well, of course he wasn't.

Even Darren Pye isn't stupid enough to stay hanging around where he'd just mugged someone.'

No, he wasn't that stupid. And maybe he'd think it'd be a good idea to get away until the heat died down. Maybe he'd look at what he'd nicked and see he'd got a winning ticket, a ticket that'd take him out of the country today. And maybe he'd decide to use that ticket.

Looking down at her mum's bruised and bloodied face, Rose really, really hoped that he did.

The Doctor arrived back at the estate. He went straight up to Rose's door, and rang the bell. After a few moments, he opened the letter box and shouted through, 'Anyone home?'

But still no one answered. The Doctor shoved at the door, but it was locked. He peered through the letter box. No sign of life. So he left.

A couple of minutes later, he was outside Mickey's door. No problems gaining entry here, the Quevvils' violent approaches had seen to that. He knocked anyway, calling out, 'Anyone home?' as he breezed in.

'In here,' came Mickey's voice, and the Doctor went through into the bedroom. Mickey was sitting by the computer, his leg propped up on the bed.

'What d'ya do to yourself?' asked the Doctor, gesturing at Mickey's blister-covered knee. 'And where's Rose?'

'I got shot by a porcupine,' answered Mickey. 'Bit hurt you don't remember.'

The Doctor waved a hand dismissively. 'What about

Rose? Is she all right? They didn't get her as well, did they?'

'Nah, she's fine. Thanks for the sympathy.'

The Doctor sighed. 'Next time, I'll bring a bunch of grapes. Anyway, where is she?'

Mickey shrugged. 'Last I knew, she was off out to collect up those games like you asked her.' He became suddenly serious. 'Look, there's something you should see. Might be nothing but... well, it's worrying.' He turned back to the computer, clicked the mouse a couple of times, and pushed back the chair so the Doctor could get close enough to see.

On the screen were the words 'KILL ALIEN'S FOR REAL ONLY £50'.

'Illiterates,' muttered the Doctor, taking over the mouse from Mickey and scrolling down.

There was a picture of a Mantodean, seemingly a screengrab from the game, and more text: 'kill alien's. this game let's you shoot alein's for real. they are giant insect's and EVIL. you can kill them. this is GARANTEED. Email alienkiller1984@mail.net'.

The Doctor thumped a fist on the desk. 'Idiots!' he said. 'If someone starts sending these games all over the country – all over the world – we'll have no chance of collecting them all. Still, let's hope no one realises this is actually the truth. Knowing humans, they'd be flocking up...'

Mickey cleared his throat. 'I think they do think it's the truth, though. The people who'll be reading this, anyway.

I was just sort of browsing, you see…'

The Doctor was already hitting the back button. 'Alien bondage ring?' he said, incredulously.

'I didn't think there'd really be sites about it!' said Mickey wretchedly. 'Er… anyone you know?'

The Doctor shut down the site with a decisive click. 'Ridiculous humans,' he said. 'I'm going to find Rose. We're stopping this now.'

Dilys's Martin gave Rose a lift home, but by the time she got back, she was exhausted. She'd been so worried about her mum, thinking that she was on some distant planet, going to be killed by aliens. The adrenalin had been pumping something rotten. Now – well, she was still worried about her mum, hurt and in hospital, and she was still worried about the whole thing, the aliens and the games and the people being killed – but the adrenalin had drained away, leaving her ready for a sit-down and a cup of tea.

She didn't notice the Doctor sitting outside her front door until she was nearly on top of him. 'Hello,' she said. 'You got away from the porcupines all right then, did you?'

He gave her a *yes, obviously* look. 'D'you do it then?' he said. 'D'you get all the games?'

She leaned over him and put her key in the lock. 'No. I haven't got any of them.'

'Why not?' he said, following her inside.

She gave a big sigh. 'You'll never believe it. My mum

had one of those holiday tickets.'

He looked concerned at that. 'Did you stop her going?'

She shook her head. 'It's all right. Well, it's sort of all right. She didn't go. She got beaten up instead. She's in hospital.' And she explained everything she'd been doing.

To her surprise, the Doctor didn't seem very sympathetic. She hadn't expected a lot, but a bit of 'poor Rose, what you must've been through' would have been nice.

'So you didn't collect up any of the games,' he said. 'You didn't even try, not even when you knew she was OK.'

Her eyes blazed. 'My *mum* was in *hospital*.'

He shrugged. 'Hospital's where they look after people. You knew she was safe. You could've stuck with the plan, maybe saved some lives. But you went to the hospital instead.'

She was so mad she could hardly get the words out. How could he not understand? Her mum was in hospital! To carry on worrying about some abstract threat when your own mum was in hospital! But a bit of her, deep inside, realised she was getting so angry because she knew, in a way, that he was right. 'Sometimes you're just not human!' she yelled. And he raised his eyebrows as if to say, 'D'uh!'

She grabbed her bag. 'I'm off to collect up these games then,' she said, her voice barely less angry than before.

The Doctor stood up. 'Good. I'll come with you.'

Her hand was actually on the door handle when the phone rang. She hesitated.

'Leave it,' said the Doctor.

She might have done, if he hadn't said that. But she was feeling contrary now, and anyway, it might be the hospital – which was important.

She weaved past the Doctor, back to the kitchen, and picked up the phone. Behind her, she heard the door slam, and knew he'd gone without her. Let him, she thought, while at the same time being just a bit terrified that she'd never see him again. But a few moments later she was haring down the steps after him, yelling at the top of her voice.

'Doctor! Doctor!' she cried, and before she'd gone two floors down he'd heard her and raced back up. All his disapproval had gone in the face of her distress, and he was the comforting best friend again, ready to take charge.

'What is it?' he asked, gripping her shoulders.

She shook her head, not sure, but as they raced back up to the flat she attempted to explain. 'Thought it was a dirty phone call. Heavy breathing and stuff. 'S not. I... I don't know. See what you think.'

They were back in the kitchen, and she jammed the handset into its holder and pressed the button for speakerphone.

It sounded like a man, a young man. There was heavy breathing, but it was the deep, ragged breaths of terror. There were gasps and what sounded like sobs catching in the throat. Just those few sounds, but so much fear.

'What is it?' asked Rose, sure she knew the answer now, but unwilling to suggest it.

'Your phone got nicked,' said the Doctor. 'So did a holiday ticket. Stands to reason the same person's got both of 'em still. So they get carried off to this alien planet, forced to play this –' his face hardened and he spat out the word – 'game.'

'But phoning here – no, don't tell me,' said Rose, 'this was the last place I called, and somehow he's knocked the redial, or the speed dial or something. That's what's happened.'

'Shh,' said the Doctor, pointing at the phone, and Rose hurriedly shut up and listened. Another sound could be heard, a loud chattering, clicking noise. The strangled sobs were getting faster, and there were choked grunts from deep in the throat, as if someone was desperately trying to form words but couldn't. The chattering sound got louder, closer to the phone.

Then there was a *schnick* noise, like a giant pair of scissors slamming shut. And then there was a soft, heavy thud.

Then the line went dead.

Rose pulled up a kitchen chair, sat down. 'I wanted that to happen,' she said. 'When I heard what he'd done to my mum, I wanted that to happen. I wanted him to be made to play that stupid alien game, I wanted him to be scared, so scared, like my mum was when he was hitting her. I wanted him to be killed like that, have his head chopped off by an alien. I wanted all of that.'

The Doctor sat down beside her. 'It's all right,' he said. 'Wanting it to happen didn't cause it. It was the Quevvils who killed Darren Pye, not you. You don't have to feel guilty.'

She turned to him, anguished. 'You don't understand. I don't feel guilty. I don't know what I feel. You know how you say, "I wouldn't wish that on my worst enemy"? Well, I'm still not sure that I wouldn't. Cos I feel sick inside, but part of me's still glad he suffered.'

'There you go, being human again,' said the Doctor. He put an arm around Rose, and hugged her to him. 'It's not fair, is it, when we're forced into pitying someone we hate. Feels like the world's turned topsy-turvy. But it's all right. You're still allowed to hate them. As long as you don't gloat at their downfall, that's all.'

Her mouth twitched into a lopsided smile. 'If you say so.'

He nodded. 'I do.'

The Doctor sat back, and Rose fished out a hankie and blew her nose hard. She suddenly realised she hadn't told him everything that had happened. 'Mickey got hurt,' she said. 'I should check he's OK.'

'I know, I've seen him,' said the Doctor. 'He'll be fine. Might've been a different story if the beam had hit him full on, but it must've only grazed him as the teleport took you out of there. He'll just be hobbling for a few weeks. And talking of hobbling… time we were doing the rounds, trying to pick up a few of these games.'

Rose took a deep breath, and stood up. 'All right,' she said. 'Let's go.'

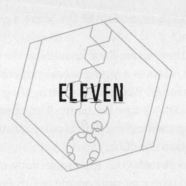

ELEVEN

They decided on a cover story. Not the best cover story in the world, but better than just turning up on someone's doorstep and demanding they give you their games console.

Rose announced she was going to pass herself off as a trading standards official, come to collect up the dangerous games which had been known to catch fire and burn down people's flats. She would tie back her hair and call herself 'Susan', or 'Pamela', or something equally sensible and trustworthy.

The Doctor pointed out that her face had been on 'Missing' posters around the estate and the surrounding areas for a year, a lot of people either knew her or knew her by sight, and anyway, why would they be less likely to trust an honest-looking, loose-haired nineteen-year-old called Rose than someone who was obviously pretending to be something she wasn't?

Rose conceded the point.

'Dumb humans!' yelled the Doctor.

Mickey looked almost nervous. 'That's not the worst of it…'

The Doctor looked at him. 'You're not telling me someone's done something even more stupid?'

'Er… yeah,' said Mickey. 'Looks like they have.' He started to click through screens on the computer. 'I've been at this since you left. Searching around, seeing what I could find out. This only went live a couple of hours ago, as far as I can tell. It's not easy to find. You go through all these links, passwords and stuff. But I got there.' He preened slightly.

'Well done, who's a clever boy,' said Rose. 'Now, are you gonna tell us what you found?'

Mickey clicked Return, and sat back.

It started with a message posted on a forum. 'It would be gr8 if game's were real if you shot someone and they were really DEAD!!!' It was signed by alienkiller1984.

'That's the bloke who runs that other site,' said the Doctor.

'But it's only the start,' said Mickey, scrolling down the thread.

'There are so manny people Id like to see DEAD. But not go to prison 4 it!!!! It would be GR8 if you could send them on holiday and they never came home but were KILLED!!!! Do you agree.'

Rose inhaled sharply.

The text 'Do you agree' was hyperlinked. 'That's where the trail starts,' said Mickey. 'Finally, you get a phone number.' He gestured to a notepad, where a mobile number had been scribbled down. 'You want someone dead – this person's prepared to sell you a winning scratchcard. Treat them to a holiday. They never come back. No blame attached.' He shivered.

The Doctor picked up Mickey's mobile off the desk without asking. He walked into the other room. Rose and Mickey looked at each other. 'It's sick, isn't it?' said Mickey.

She nodded, not really able to bring herself to add to that. Totally sick. Utterly sick. Lose all faith in human nature sick. 'How's the knee?'

'Sore,' he said. 'Don't know how I'm going to cope, to be honest.'

She grimaced in sympathy.

'What I really need is someone to help me out – look after me, put me to bed, that sort of thing.'

'Shame I'm busy saving the world,' she said. 'I'll phone social services, if you like. They can sent round some nice old granny to give you a bed bath.'

Mickey grinned. 'Oh, what a shame the Doctor's using my phone.'

'Oh, look, he's finished,' said Rose as the Doctor walked back in. But their banter was cut short by the expression on the Doctor's face. 'What is it?' Rose said.

'Five hundred quid,' said the Doctor. 'That's how much death costs off the Internet. Not much more than a wide-screen telly.'

'You spoke to someone?' asked Rose.

The Doctor nodded. 'And it didn't sound as if I was the first to call. I reckon your mum's not the only one who's been mugged for her winning scratchcard.'

Rose thought of her mum, lying bruised and bloody in a hospital bed. 'We've got to stop this,' she said.

'Well, yeah,' said the Doctor. 'That's the general idea.' He reached out a hand and squeezed her arm, a comforting gesture that belied the very slight sarcasm of his words. Rose noticed Mickey's face. He didn't like it; didn't like their closeness. She understood, but didn't have time now to worry about Mickey's feelings.

'We've got to stop it at the source,' the Doctor was saying. 'It's spreading out all over the place down here. Look, this Internet stuff has only just started. Nothing stolen before this afternoon, far as we know. Earliest anyone can get anything by post is tomorrow morning. We've got to get to the planet where it's all happening before then, stop it there. Then it won't matter who's got the games, who wins the holidays.'

Rose dragged her attention back to the conversation. 'What, you found out where this planet is?' she asked. 'Can we dash off to the rescue?'

The Doctor's face hardened. 'No,' he said, clenching his fists. 'I got its name, but it doesn't mean a thing.'

'You could pay 500 quid to this bloke and go on the holiday,' Mickey suggested, and Rose was fairly sure she didn't really detect just a hint of malice, just the tiniest indication that Mickey wouldn't mind too much if the Doctor went off 'on holiday' and never came back.

'There's an idea,' said the Doctor.

'What, really?' said Mickey, slightly incredulous.

The Doctor soon deflated him. 'Not your actual idea, obviously,' he said. 'That's pretty stupid. But it's given me an idea… If we could just get hold of one of those holiday scratchcards. With the Quevvils' teleportation technology, it'd be bound to have a directional circuit in it… I could plug that into the TARDIS…' He bounded over to the door. 'Come on, you two.' Mickey gestured at his knee. 'Come on, then, just Rose. I need your life savings. We're buying scratchcards until we get one that wins the holiday.'

At which point Rose remembered her meeting with Dilys by the Quevvils' booth. She put her hand in her pocket and pulled out a small cardboard rectangle. 'What, like this one?' she said. 'Didn't really seem important earlier…'

She wasn't sure from the Doctor's expression whether he wanted to smack her or kiss her.

'Nice one, Rose,' said Mickey.

The Doctor left Mickey with instructions to keep sowing Internet dissent about *Death to Mantodeans*, make it seem as undesirable as possible, see if their rumour about the consoles catching fire could spread any further.

Mickey suggested actually setting fire to one and calling the local papers, but changed his mind halfway through explaining the plan when he realised that it would be his flat at risk, and with his knee he couldn't actually run away if things went wrong.

'Plus, it's another stupid idea,' commented the Doctor, not unkindly.

'And look after yourself,' said Rose. 'Oh, and could you make sure Mrs Burton gets her shopping basket on wheels back.'

'Yeah, course,' said Mickey, sounding a bit worried. 'But you're coming back, ain't ya?'

'Course we are,' said Rose. But the thing was, when you went off into time and space in the TARDIS, you were never entirely sure.

Mickey hobbled across to the front door to see them off. 'I'd stick a wedge under it or something till you can get it fixed,' said the Doctor. 'Don't forget that the Quevvils know where you live.'

'You said you smashed their teleport system!' said Rose.

'They might fix it!' replied the Doctor.

'Thanks for the cheerful thought,' said Mickey. 'I'll sleep so soundly tonight now.'

Rose heard the door shut behind them as they started down the stairs. 'We're gonna be able to stop this, aren't we?' she asked the Doctor.

'It'll be a cinch,' he replied.

'No more humans getting their heads bitten off by aliens?'

'And no more aliens getting shot by humans,' said the Doctor. 'Don't worry. We'll stop it, no problem.'

* * *

A figure had slipped into the shadows of a doorway as the Doctor and Rose left Mickey's flat. Now it left its hiding place and peered round the corner to watch them as they went down the stairs: the tall, arrogant bloke and the mouthy tart. He'd wipe the smiles off their faces. They weren't going to get in his way again.

'You ain't gonna stop this,' grunted Darren Pye, spitting after the retreating figures. 'I'm the one who's gonna stop *you.*'

TWELVE

'*I love you, Robert.*' *The beautiful girl with the long blonde hair who looked a bit like Suzie Price was gazing at him in adoration. 'I've been watching you, couldn't keep my eyes off you. I watched how you dealt with those terrible aliens. The way you grabbed that iron bar and used it like a sword, the way you fenced with that alien and drove him off… You must be a master swordsman!'*

Robert smiled modestly, indicating that he'd never tried before, it had just come naturally.

And it came just as naturally to put his arms around her; the most natural thing in the world to lean down as she leaned up and they put their lips together and kissed, their first kiss, his first kiss, the softest, most beautiful kiss in the world…

But she was sitting over the other side of the room and had barely looked in his direction, and when she had she hadn't noticed him, and she'd probably heard his mum call him 'Bobbles'…

And then the leader of the aliens, the one that Robert had defeated in battle, had taken off his mask and underneath he had the head of a porcupine

– had taken off his mask, and said, in his cold, deep voice, 'I am your father, Robert.'

And Robert knew that it had ever been their destiny to meet in this way, and that he must destroy his – mother *– father as the ultimate triumph of good over evil.*

And then he might get another kiss.

Mickey looked around the lounge, and finally picked up a TV mag. 'Won't be needing this any more,' he murmured, casting a rueful eye over at the gap where only that morning the television had stood. Then he slowly made his way back to the front door, and, crouching down with a lot of yelps of pain – although probably not as many as if anyone had been present to potentially offer sympathy – wedged the magazine between the frame and the door. It probably wouldn't stand much, but would prevent anyone bursting in on him. He glanced up at the wall, where a large red sign instructed people to STOP. Shame aliens didn't pay any attention to that.

He had taken two shuffling steps back from the door when he heard a noise on the other side. The aliens? Mickey hurriedly looked round for a weapon. But no, a second's concentration and he realised it was footsteps. Human footsteps. The Doctor and Rose, having forgotten something? No, it was only one person. The burglar, returning for more?

Mickey kept still and silent. Inside he was laughing and

pointing at himself for the paranoia, but exposure to the Doctor had had an effect. There were some scary things out there. 'Don't have nightmares,' *Crimewatch* always said, but they were trying to persuade people it was statistically unlikely for the awful things they were showing to happen to any particular audience member, and when you'd been there and done that on what seemed like a regular basis now, you stopped believing the platitudes.

Were the footsteps going to pass his door? No. They stopped right outside it.

And tried the handle.

A legitimate visitor would knock at this point, or call out or something.

No one knocked, and no one called out. Instead, they tried shoving the door again. The door opened a centimetre or so, the magazine beginning to scrunch up. A rough, male voice said, 'Open up, Smith.' Darren Pye.

Mickey didn't say a word. He began to back away, as quietly as he could, looking for something else he could use to keep the door shut.

'I know you're in there, Smith. I know your freaky friends brought some of them games here, and I want 'em.'

'Well, you can't have them,' called back Mickey, forgetting he was pretending not to be there.

It sounded as if Darren was giving the door a kicking. Amazingly, the magazine was still wedged tightly beneath it, preventing it from opening, but any moment he'd have it off its hinges.

But then the noise stopped. Mickey suddenly stood up

straight, alerted by a feeling that he couldn't quite place. A tingle in the air, and for some reason Pancake Day came to mind... He heard a shout of alarm from outside the door, probably the nearest anyone had ever heard Darren Pye get to shock and fear.

Then Mickey realised: this was what it had felt like just before the aliens – the Quevvils – had burst into his flat. The Doctor's warning had been right; they must have been able to fix their teleport system, and they'd just materialised the other side of his front door.

They'd be after the Doctor. Had to be. But maybe they still thought Mickey was an expert; maybe with the Doctor not here they'd try to kidnap Mickey again... Or, worse, maybe they'd worked out that Mickey wasn't an expert, and they wouldn't want to risk him spreading details of their plans or their underground base or their true nature...

There was no other exit from his flat. Even in full health he couldn't hope to outmanoeuvre the Quevvils and their flying quills and their laser guns; with his dodgy knee he had no chance. Mickey hurried back as fast as he could, eager to find a hiding place. But then he heard voices from outside.

'How on Earth did you do that?' yelled Darren Pye.

Then came the voice of a Quevvil: 'This human has witnessed our materialisation! He must be destroyed!'

Mickey froze, waiting for the hiss of the laser beam, the scream of the dying man. But it didn't come.

'No!' yelled Darren Pye. 'I can help you!'

There was a pause, then a Quevvil said, 'Explain.'

Darren was gabbling now. 'I know what you are, right? I know what you're doing. I heard those freaks talking. You're aliens, right, and you want to kill these insect things. That's cool. I saw you appear before, out of thin air like that. I want to help.'

A Quevvil – Mickey had no idea if it was the same or a different one – said, 'You have not yet explained how you intend to help us.'

'I've already sorted it. Spreading these things over the country. Getting people who know what they're doing.'

And the unsurprise of the century: Darren Pye was the dealer. The death dealer. The one who would send your anyone to their death for less than the price of a telly. And thinking of tellies, he probably had a fair idea where Mickey's had gone too; why else would he have been hanging around here to hear the Doctor and Rose talking, to see the Quevvils appear...

And the Quevvil replied, 'We have already located the person we need. We have come here to fetch him.'

'What, that Doctor freak?' said Darren. 'He's not here.'

Mickey didn't know what happened next, but Darren let out a yelp. 'No! Look, I said I could help you. I'll tell you where he is. All I want is that you make me your sole dealer on Earth. People'll pay good money for this stuff. I just want a cut. Look, do we have a deal?'

There was a pause, then a Quevvil said, 'Yes. Tell us where this "Doctor freak" is.'

'Right. Yeah. Right. He's gone to your planet, him and

that little cow. He's got a thing called a tarpit or something. He's plugging one of your cards in it and it'll take him there.'

There was another pause.

'We must warn Frinel,' said one Quevvil.

'We must return to Toop,' said the voice of another.

'What about this human? Shall I kill him?'

There was a yell from Darren Pye. 'We had a deal! I said I'd help you!'

The Quevvil spoke again. 'No. Bring him with us. We cannot afford to leave behind a human who knows the truth, but if this human wants to help us... he can play the game.'

There was another yell from Darren, abruptly cut off. Mickey shivered. Had they killed him after all? But no, there was the lemony scent in the air again, and the fizzy feeling that made his hair stand on end.

He left it for a couple of minutes, but couldn't stand the suspense any longer than that. He limped to the front door, and put his ear against it. Not a sound. He pulled away the crumpled magazine, and eased open the door. No one was outside: no humans, no aliens.

Mickey slammed the door, shoved the magazine under it again, stumbled back into the lounge and collapsed on a chair. His knee was hurting like crazy, but all he could think about was the Doctor and Rose. The monsters knew they were on their way. They'd be waiting for them. And there was no way on Earth he could let them know about it.

* * *

They were hand in hand, and they almost jogged back to the TARDIS. It was a time machine, but somehow time still seemed of the essence.

The Doctor, annoyingly, hadn't told Rose his plan. This either meant that he didn't have one, or he just expected her to do what he asked her, when he asked her, without worrying about silly little things like explanations or reasons for it. But she didn't have to put up with that. 'What's the plan then?' she asked as they came up to the TARDIS, reasoning she might as well know the worst sooner rather than later. Just because it was the Doctor's time machine, that didn't mean she had to play entirely by his rules.

'I'm gonna try an' home in on this Mantodean stronghold. Rescue anyone still in there. Then find where they're holding the people ready to play the game. Rescue them. Persuade the Quevvils not to do this any more. When we don't succeed, do something clever which means they can't do it whether they want to or not.'

'Great,' she said. 'I approve.'

'I'm glad you approve,' the Doctor replied, getting out his TARDIS key.

'How're we going to do all that then?' she asked. 'Bribe them with salt?'

The Doctor had earlier seemed not entirely impressed by her salt brainwave. She'd explained it in detail while they'd been trooping round all the flats.

'Well, I remembered this thing about how porcupines go mad for it,' she'd explained. 'They chew stuff to bits if someone's just touched it with sweaty hands, that's how much they love it. So I figured…'

The Doctor had interrupted her. 'These aren't porcu-pines! Porcupines don't, contrary to popular belief, shoot their quills at you. They don't walk upright. They don't carry little laser guns. And they don't, whatever David Attenborough might tell you, kidnap human beings and teleport them to an alien planet!'

Rose shrugged. 'Well, I knew it was a long shot…'

He'd grinned then. 'A bloomin' brilliant one!' And he'd given her a great big hug, swinging her off her feet. 'I'll never let anyone call you a dumb human again.'

'What, you mean they –'

'Nah,' he'd interrupted again, laughing, and he took her hand and led her off down the street.

'Nah,' he said again now. 'We're going to figure that out when we get there. Easier that way. I hate having to keep rejigging a plan just cos there was something we didn't know about before we arrived.'

'Yeah, right,' said Rose. 'You've just got this seat-of-the-pants thing going. You'd get all bored if you'd got it sorted beforehand.'

He just smiled at that, as he pushed open the blue dou-ble doors; didn't confirm or deny.

Rose was sort of used to coming into the TARDIS now, in the same way Alexander Graham Bell's friends must have grown used to the miracle of being called up on the telephone after the first few times, but she still got a rush from it, the casual wandering into a wonderful alien en-vironment, a machine that was, amazingly, bigger on the inside than the outside. That would have been astounding enough in itself, even without the whole 'travel to any-where and anywhen' thing.

The Doctor held out a hand for the winning scratch-card as they walked up the ramp into the dark control room, and she pulled it out of her jeans pocket again, hop-ing the slight crease it in wouldn't have harmed whatever strange technology it was concealing.

She passed it over, and the Doctor stuck the card into a slot in the console. The TARDIS always seemed to have exactly what was needed. Rose suspected that it somehow adapted itself to the Doctor's requirements, but she'd never managed to catch it out; never managed to spot something that she knew hadn't been there before, or found anything to be absent that had previously been present.

'Won't be long,' said the Doctor.

Rose hoped so, you really didn't want too much time to reflect before plunging into deadly danger. The Doctor flicked a few switches, and the thin column in the middle of the console began to pulse up and down, bathing the room in blue-green light. That meant they were in flight. That they were, as far as she could understand it, more or less nowhere. Travelling in the TARDIS was more like the Quevvils' teleportation than a rocket to the moon: you didn't have to take a detour round Saturn or risk getting stuck in a spaceship jam at the edge of the Milky Way, you just... Well, actually, she'd leave the details to the Doctor. Just take it on trust for now.

The Doctor was mooching round the console, his

hands in his pockets, occasionally peering down at something. He did not thrive on inactivity. 'Be there any second,' he said.

'Good,' said Rose, 'I –' But she suddenly found herself flying across the room. The TARDIS had lurched violently, like it had given a sudden enormous hiccup. She grabbed at one of the strange sculptures that decorated the room, a sort of Y-shaped thing that looked like a cross between a tree and a statue, and it arrested her flight. Using it for support, she managed to drag herself back to her feet.

'What was that?' she asked, shaken.

The Doctor was examining the console. 'We were repelled by something.'

'The force field around the Mantodean stronghold!' Rose realised. 'No teleporting, no TARDIS.'

The Doctor nodded. 'So that's Plan A out of the window.'

'Well, we were making it up as we went along,' said Rose, to sort of comfort him. 'We've landed somewhere, anyway.'

'Mm,' said the Doctor, getting his sonic screwdriver out of his pocket as if to check he still had it, then putting it back in again. 'I expect it's gone into default mode, taken us to exactly where the winning-card holders materialise. But the best way to find out –'

'Is to go out,' completed Rose.

The Doctor opened the TARDIS doors, and Rose followed him outside

THIRTEEN

There were about fifteen people in the room. *There were fourteen now, fourteen exactly.* There always seemed to be about fifteen, because as fast as they took people away, new ones appeared. When the people materialised out of thin air they were usually upset and confused. If you'd been there for a while, you had to explain what was happening. Not that you really knew. Sometimes people had barely arrived before Percy the Porcupine came in and took them away. Sometimes, like Robert, you could be there for hours. No one knew where they took you, but everyone was scared, no one wanted to be picked.

His mum had done this really embarrassing thing, crying and screaming for them to take her instead of him, trying to throw herself in front of him and stop the monsters from getting near him.

Some people said they probably ate you.

And they had picked her –

– and that was real.

Robert didn't believe what the people said. He didn't believe that was what was happening.

'You won't hurt him! I won't let you take him!'

Robert didn't think the porcupines could really tell the humans apart, either; they weren't picking or leaving behind anyone in particular; it was just chance. Some people obviously thought they picked whoever was nearest to hand, and they tried hiding behind everyone else. Robert despised people like that, the cowards. But then other people pushed him to the back, tried to protect him because he was the youngest there, and although he told them not to he didn't push them out of the way, didn't yell, 'No, take me instead!' Not like his mum had.

He was desperate to be brave, desperate to be a hero, but it was his mum who'd been the real hero.

And heroes always came back. They always beat the odds against them.

At the moment, there was Robert, and there was the blonde girl and her mum. The girl's name was Sarah, not that she spoke to him, because girls didn't even in life-or-death situations, but he'd heard her mum call her that. Sarah's face swapped between the most perfect sneer and the most gorgeous pout Robert had ever seen. She'd cried a bit, at first, but now just looked bored. There were four couples at various degrees of agedness: the Nkomos (old: probably in their thirties), the Catesbys (very old: probably forties), the Snows (ancient: fifty or so) and the Atallas (in their sixties: practically dead). They were all new arrivals. Everyone kept out of the way of the Snows, who didn't seem to realise what was happening and kept trying to insist that they must talk to someone in charge.

There was a man called Daniel Goldberg, whose wife had been taken away, and who now just sat in a corner crying, and another man, probably aged twenty or so, who was wearing a suit and tie and had been virtually in hysterics since he arrived. He'd said his name was George, as far as he could be understood through all the whimpering and screaming, and Robert thought he was pathetic. He hoped he'd be taken next. Then there was an old granny called Mrs Pobjoy, who said it was just like the war and kept trying to organise sing-songs. At the moment, she was giving everyone a rousing chorus of 'Pack up your troubles in your old kit bag', but Robert really couldn't see that they had anything to smile, smile, smile about, although they might do if she stopped.

Suddenly a loud grating, rasping noise began echoing around the room. It sounded like some great engine grinding into life, and everyone started in terror. 'It's the mincing machine!' shouted George. 'They're going to eat us all!' He tried to grab Mrs Nkomo to pull her in front of him. Mr Nkomo pushed him back and looked as if he was about to punch George. Robert didn't blame him.

But then the thing appeared, and grabbed everyone's attention. If it was a mincing machine, it was stranger – although less scary – than any Robert could imagine. The thing arrived out of nowhere: a blue box, taller than a man, with a flashing light on top and little windows high up on the sides – sort of like a small blue shed, only it had the words 'Police Public Call Box' written on it.

Everyone stood staring at it for what seemed like a very long time, but was really only seconds. Mrs Atalla said to her husband, 'It's a police box. Like they used to have,' and her husband said, 'I remember.' They stared at it, standing hand in hand, which was pretty disgusting for people of their age.

Then the doors of the police box opened, and a man stepped out.

He was a tall man who looked a bit like some of the trendier teachers at school – he had really short hair, and was wearing a really cool battered leather jacket that Robert coveted immediately. If Robert's dad ever did turn up, he'd like him to be a man who looked like that. And, actually, he'd quite like him to be a man who appeared out of nowhere in a blue box as well.

And then the second person came out of the box, and Robert forgot all about the man, and all about Sarah the blonde sneering girl, and about his mum, and even all about Suzie Price, because this was the girl he was going to love for ever. She was totally beautiful and utterly cool and just, well, perfect. She was probably about eighteen or nineteen, but that wouldn't matter because he was really mature for his age, and she had dark blonde hair past her shoulders and a wide, smiling mouth that was even more desirable than Sarah the blonde sneering girl's, and as she left the blue box her eyes met his and she smiled, and he knew that she felt it too, the connection between them.

The girl pushed past her companion and headed straight for Robert. She had eyes for no one else. And she held out her hands towards him, and he took them in his, and she said just the one word, 'Hello,' and then she grinned at him.

He said breathlessly, 'I'm Robert.'

She said, 'I know. We've come here for you, Robert. I've come here for you. Because you're special. I've been wanting to meet you for so long.'

He said, 'I've been wanting to meet you too, although I hardly dared to believe that there was someone so beautiful in the world.'

She leaned towards him, she was going to take him in her arms, and he stood strong and tall and closed his eyes, and said, 'I don't even know your name…'

He opened his eyes. The girl was standing behind the tall man, in the doorway of the police box. 'All right,' said the man in a northern accent, looking round at everyone, 'We're the rescue party.'

And Robert smiled for real.

The room they'd landed in was totally grim, a bleak concrete shell. A group of people were huddled in one corner, staring at the Doctor and Rose: mainly adults, but a couple of kids too, one boy and one girl. They all had small metal discs stuck to their foreheads, like Mrs Hall and the lad they'd seen in the game.

'We're gonna take you home,' said Rose, stepping forward. There were disbelieving smiles from the crowd; one man threw himself on the ground and started weeping.

A moustached man pushed himself to the front of the

group. 'Are you in charge here?' he said. 'I have a serious complaint to make!'

Next to him, bizarrely, an elderly woman began to sing, 'There'll be bluebirds over the white cliffs of Dover…'

'Don't think you'll find any bluebirds in England, love,' said the Doctor. 'Now, blue boxes, on the other hand…' He gave an exaggerated, ringmaster's gesture towards the TARDIS. 'If I could trouble you all to walk this way…'

The door to the room thudded open, and two Quevvils stood in the doorway, with several more behind them. Their heads were down and their quills bristling.

'Inside, now!' barked the Doctor, but the instant they sprang towards the TARDIS, before the poor people in the corner had taken even a single step, a barrage of quills soared through the air, tinkling on to the concrete floor at their feet. A few stuck into the sides of the TARDIS.

'That was just a warning!' called the lead Quevvil, as they all froze on the spot.

The first two Quevvils slowly came into the room.

And with them was a human. A human Rose recognised. It was Darren Pye.

'What on Earth is he doing here?' she cried out to the Doctor. 'I thought he was dead!'

'No such luck,' said the Doctor. 'He's the one who was nicking the games and selling them on the Internet.'

And she realised the rest, wondered why she hadn't worked it out before. They'd heard someone outside, thought it was the person who'd nicked Mickey's telly.

He'd have heard everything they said, about the games, about the holidays, about the aliens. And he went down the stairs and met Jackie and had taken her ticket and her phone. Wouldn't have used the ticket himself, not knowing what it represented. Sold it straight away, and before you could say Jack Robinson the poor guy who'd bought it had ended up dying here, on this planet.

'I thought I recognised the voice when he offered to send my unwanted old aunt a winning scratchcard for 500 quid,' said the Doctor. He raised his voice. 'Must have been a bummer when you found out how much you could get for them, when you'd already sold Jackie's ticket – and the phone. What did you get that time? Twenty quid? Thirty?'

Darren Pye just scowled at them. But one of the kids, the boy, started forward. 'Johnny Deans,' he cried. 'He said he'd bought his ticket off someone down the pub for £30, and they threw in a mobile too. He was only here for five minutes before they took him.' The boy paused, and looked at his watch. 'That was about two and a half hours ago.'

'That'd be about right,' said Rose quietly. She'd known Johnny Deans from school, not properly or anything, but she knew who he was. Darren Pye used to beat him up, she remembered. Ultimate act of bullying, this. Johnny probably wondered why his old enemy was doing him a favour. Now she was thinking of those desperate, dying sounds on the telephone. Thinking of how she hadn't been able to feel sorry about the death. Now she knew it had been someone else dying, someone she'd no grudge against, her stomach suddenly flipped with guilt.

The remaining Quevvils had entered the room; there were now five in all, far too many for the Doctor or Rose to risk trying anything. The lead Quevvil pointed at Rose. 'Prepare the human,' it said. Which didn't sound good at all.

The Doctor jumped in front of her. 'You're not doing anything to her,' he said.

'You have no choice,' replied the Quevvil. He was smiling smugly at the Doctor. 'You will play the game for us and that human –' he indicated Rose – 'will be your carrier. If you resist, we will kill that one, and one of these humans –' now he pointed at the cowering group in the corner – 'will act as your carrier instead.'

'Just take her!' yelled someone from the group – the young man who'd been sobbing on the floor. Rose developed an instant and overwhelming dislike for him. 'Leave us alone, please!'

The Doctor hadn't moved, but the Quevvils' quills were beginning to bristle again. Better to take her chance with being a 'carrier' than a pointed death here and now. Rose stepped forwards, trying not to look nervous. A young, hesitant voice called out, 'Don't worry. It doesn't really hurt.' She turned to see the boy who'd spoken before pointing at the metal disc in the middle of his forehead. So that's what they were going to do to her first. She gave the boy a smile, thanking him for the comfort, trying to show she wasn't afraid.

As she passed the Doctor, he suddenly swept her into a great hug. For a moment it scared her: perhaps he really did think this was goodbye, perhaps he didn't think he could rescue her... But then she felt him pressing something into her hand, and she realised the over-the-top embrace was just a distraction. As the Quevvils shouted at them to stop, and the Doctor drew back from her, Rose hurriedly shoved the Doctor's sonic screwdriver up the left sleeve of her top.

Two of the Quevvils came with her, and led her down a depressingly grey corridor. She made no effort to get away – hard to run from creatures who could spray needle-sharp quills down the length of the corridor, and anyway, where would she run to?

At the end of the corridor was a door, and the Quevvils took her into a room.

The first thing she noticed was the window. She'd known that Toop was a desert planet, and she'd seen bits of it on the screen via *Death to Mantodeans*, but it was still a shock to come face to face with it. Somehow she'd expected a desert to resemble an enormous version of Southend, only with fewer ice-cream sellers and more oases, but it was nothing like.

The sky... the sky wasn't a glorious holiday blue, it was a dull blue, a grey-blue, so pale as to be almost colourless. The sun was harshly white: glaringly bright, but lifeless. And even the ground disappointed, she could tell it wasn't deep, soft sand, the sort you'd make castles out of – or even ride a camel across – it was more like dead ground: dusty and yellow and parched. And it was bleak. All she could see in the distance was a single structure, a dull ochre mound that did actually look a bit like someone had upturned a bucket of sand and produced a truncated cone with one tap of their spade. She reckoned that must be the Mantodean place. Only a few kilometres away. A local war.

The Quevvil holding her snarled, and she started. But it was snarling at the view. 'A world blighted by Mantodeans,' it said. 'But not for much longer…'

'Have you ever thought of, you know, just trying to be friends?' said Rose. The Quevvils ignored that, and the second one grabbed hold of her arm. 'Ow!' she said. 'Or you could just put up curtains so they don't spoil your view…' They took no notice of that, either.

There were several workbenches in the room, and one Quevvil led – dragged – her over to one on the far side, away from the window. It kept hold of her, as the other picked up a metal disc, and held it to Rose's head. She instinctively tried to back away, but only succeeded in standing on the foot of the Quevvil holding her. It pushed her forward impatiently, and the second Quevvil then slammed the disc against her forehead.

The disc had little claws sticking out of it on one side, and to her horror it didn't stick on to her forehead like she'd expected, it stuck *into* her forehead. She could feel the claws grab hold, push their way into the flesh, and then clench up, as if they were making a fist. It was a horrible experience, but to her surprise the boy had been right, it didn't really hurt; just a short, sharp shock like having your ears pierced, then a nagging unpleasantness, but no actual lingering pain.

Then one of the Quevvils pressed a button on a small silver box, and the pain began.

Or maybe it wasn't pain. But it was the most unpleasant sensation. Something was happening inside her. The feeling started at the disc on her forehead and slowly spread throughout her body. It was as if tiny wires were threading themselves along every nerve. Worst of all, she couldn't react: couldn't shout or back way; couldn't move a single muscle.

The Quevvil then picked up a small metal cube. Rose realised what it was doing – this was like the beginning of the game, only she wasn't in a title sequence, they were preparing her to play for real.

The cube was on a thick metal wire, and the Quevvil hung it around her neck, twisting it so the wire encircled her like a noose. Two more wires, taken under her arms, were attached behind Rose's back. Without cutting the wire – or removing her head – it would be impossible to get rid of the cube.

She watched the Quevvil who had been holding her go over to a device on the wall, just like one she'd seen on the wall of their underground lair back in London. It spoke into it: 'Is the controller ready?'

'The controller is ready,' a voice confirmed. 'You will dispatch the carrier.'

'Understood.'

The Quevvil did something at the control panel. Rose had a split second to register the tang in the air that spoke to her of the Quevvils' teleportation devices. And then – she was somewhere else.

FOURTEEN

The man had let the wonderful girl be taken by the porcupines. Robert couldn't believe it. He'd only just met her, and she was being taken from him already.

Mind you, the man really didn't seem happy about it. He wasn't doing anything now, but from the way he looked, Robert was pretty sure he wasn't just going to accept the situation.

The tall man turned to the nearest porcupine. 'I was planning on just rescuing everyone and, you know, maybe destroying your technology so you wouldn't do it again,' he said conversationally, acting totally coolly about it all. 'If she gets hurt, though, this planet's dust. Just thought I'd mention it.'

Yeah, thought Robert. Dust. If they hurt her, he'd be there helping this man smash it all up.

The other man, the ugly one who had come in with the porcupines, snorted with laughter. 'You and whose army?'

The tall man turned to him. 'You know what, Darren? That thing I said about dust? Applies to you too. If she gets hurt.' He really looked as if he meant it, and Robert was pleased to see the ugly man – Darren – look a bit nervous.

But the porcupine didn't seem to care what the man was saying. 'Your carrier will soon be in place,' it told the tall man. 'You will come with us and play the game.'

'Yeah, you tell him,' said Darren, rallying.

The tall man actually laughed. 'If you knew how pathetic you looked!' he said to Darren. 'Trying to ally yourself with the Quevvils, cos you think they won't hurt you that way. Like they think of you as any different from the rest of the humans! You know what they call people who do that, who betray their own species, who do the "every man for himself" thing? They call them chickens.' And, to Robert's absolute delight and amazement, he began to do a chicken impression, clucking and flapping his arms.

The man called Darren looked really mad at that. 'No one calls me a chicken!' he yelled, and started forward, looking as if he was going to hit the other man. But one of the porcupines – the Quevvils? – put out a paw and stopped him.

'Be quiet, human,' it said. It turned, as another Quevvil came in the room.

'Three more carriers required, Frinel,' said the new entry. The Quevvil that had been addressed nodded. Robert's stomach tightened. Three more carriers. Three more of them to be taken away goodness knew where, for goodness knew what.

The new Quevvil came over towards them.

'Wait!' yelled the tall man. 'If I'm going to play your game for you, you don't need anyone else playing it! Shut down the connections to Earth. Don't make any more humans play the game.'

But the Quevvil called Frinel looked like he was smirking. 'Until you succeed, the game will continue to be played,' he said. 'Perhaps there is another controller out there as good as you.'

'There isn't!' said the man, sounding frustrated. 'As I told your friends before, you're not going to find a human who can play the game to the end! I'm your only chance. So it's pointless. You're sending these people to their deaths for nothing!'

There was a wail from George, and gasps from most of the women. All the husbands clasped their wives to them. Sarah's mother held her tight. But Robert was all alone. They'd all known it really, of course; all known that the people who were taken away were going to die. But they'd never been totally sure; they'd always been able to hope just a tiny bit.

Robert felt tears start to build in the corner of his eyes, an unpleasant, itchy sensation. He blinked hard.

The Quevvil came over to them. Robert tried to stand tall, to not show his fear. George was still wailing, and Robert thought he was so stupid, drawing attention to himself, that he'd be picked for certain. But the Quevvil took Mr and Mrs Nkomo and Mr Snow. The Nkomos held each other's hands tightly. Mrs Snow grabbed hold of her husband's arm and began to scream at the Quevvil, something about it being an outrage, but it was no use. What always happened, happened. The Quevvil pointed a small silver box at their foreheads, and one by one Mr Nkomo, Mrs Nkomo and Mr Snow became rigid, like statues. The discs on their foreheads began to flash red. Then the Quevvil pushed a switch on the silver box, and all three began to walk forward robotically. It would have been funny in other circumstances: the old white man and the young black couple marching stiffly in unison together, they looked as if they were on some silly kids' programme with those embarrassing presenters who pretend to be talking to you through the screen – 'Now, everyone pretend to be soldiers. Well done, that's great!' But here, no one was finding it entertaining.

Except the ugly man, Darren. He began to chortle, aping their robot walk, his eyes wide and mock-staring, his mouth doing a 'Duh, duh, duh' thing. Robert really, really wanted to hit him.

Another Quevvil appeared in the doorway. 'Toral,' it called, addressing the Quevvil with the silver box, 'a fourth carrier is required.'

'This isn't very efficient, if you ask me,' said the tall man. 'I wondered why you had to build such a long introduction into the game. Still, hopefully it's worked out for the best. I bet loads of people have switched off in boredom before it's even started.'

'Shall I use him?' said Toral, pointing at the tall man. Robert's heart leapt in fear.

Over the other side of the room, Darren was laughing, still half mimicking the stiff-armed movements of the three people already chosen. 'Yeah, use the freak,' he said. 'Show him what you do to people who threaten you, right?'

But Frinel was turning to look at the ugly man now. Robert looked at Darren too, and was filled with contempt tinged with horror – he was acting as if he was with the monsters; couldn't he see that he wasn't, that they weren't looking at him any differently to anyone else? He thought he was safe, and he wasn't.

And Frinel said to the other Quevvil, 'No. That is the controller who will bring us victory.' He raised a paw. 'Use him.' He was pointing at Darren.

It took Darren a few seconds to realise what Frinel meant. Then he began to scream. 'But I helped you! I told you what was happening. I told you about them and their spaceship! They'd have mucked up everything for you if I hadn't warned you, the Doctor freak and that little cow!'

But it made no difference. Robert tried to tear his eyes away, but his brain wouldn't process the request. Toral lifted up the silver box, but then realised that Darren didn't have a metal disc on his forehead. He gestured at the Quevvil who had come in with the request, and it grabbed hold of Darren. They left the room, a grotesque procession: three people marching inhumanly followed by a Quevvil with the control box held out at arm's length, then a struggling, ugly man in the arms of another Quevvil, then a further Quevvil following.

The tall man was gazing towards Robert and the group. His eyes seemed to be trying to reassure them, trying to distract them from the terrible sight. 'No one else, I promise,' he said, and Robert didn't know how he could possibly promise that, but he sounded so sincere that he couldn't help but believe him. 'No one else after this. I'm going to stop it.'

The door shut behind the procession. Two Quevvils were left, one of them the leader called Frinel. He turned to the tall man and said, 'Now you will come with me.' Then he turned to his fellow and said, 'And bring one of those with us.' He gestured at Robert and the others.

Everyone froze again. They'd – well, not exactly relaxed, but they'd thought it was over for now. The unlucky ones had been picked. The rest were safe, for a little while longer. But they weren't.

Robert felt people begin to back away again, not that there was anywhere further for them to back away to. George started wailing again: 'Not me! Not me!' Robert looked at him in disgust. Coward, he thought. Coward, coward.

But Robert was a coward too. He'd let other people be taken. He'd done nothing to stop it, nothing to push himself forward to save someone else even at the expense of his own life. He'd let his

don't think about Mum

He'd let other people do it instead. He was the kid, he

should be protected. He was special, he was –

But he wasn't special. He wasn't the Chosen One.

And even if he was…

He loved books like that, and telly, and films. He loved stuff where there was a Chosen One, a special person, a hero, and he loved to imagine that one day things like that would happen to him. But there was one thing he'd noticed, and that was that however much the hero seemed to risk his life, all the way through there would be other people risking their lives too, happy to give up their lives so the Chosen One, the hero, could live to fight another day, or do something clever, and everyone accepted that that was just as it should be. Often, the hero didn't even know their names. He certainly rarely gave them a second thought, after the first brief regret of the loss.

Robert knew he wasn't the hero, wasn't special. But looking at this man, the 'Doctor freak' as Darren called him, he knew that he was in the presence of someone who was.

He remembered what the man had said about no one else being taken. Well, maybe he was almost right. He was going to put a stop to all this, Robert really believed that. So maybe one more person had to go, and then everyone else would be all right: Sarah, and her mother, and old Mrs Pobjoy and the rest. And maybe the person going would be able to help the hero. Maybe be able to give their life for the hero. Maybe be part of the solution, even if they had to die. Maybe even be regretted one day by that wonderful girl, the hero's friend, because he knew the hero would rescue her somehow. She'd never know his name, but perhaps she'd shed a small tear and say, 'That boy, the last one to die. We'd never have been able to do it without his sacrifice.'

And Robert suddenly realised he'd pushed himself forward, brushing off the protesting arms of Mrs Pobjoy and Mrs Catesby, and was calling out, 'Take me.'

And they did.

To Robert's intense surprise, no one produced a little silver box and activated the disc on his forehead. He was led out of the room still under his own control, which he was extremely pleased about, although still pretty much terrified. He tried not to show that to the tall man, the hero, who was walking beside him.

The man turned to Robert. 'Hello,' he said. 'I'm the Doctor.'

'I'm Robert,' said Robert.

'That was pretty brave,' said the Doctor, as they were led down a corridor.

'Not really,' mumbled Robert, embarrassed. He didn't think the hero was supposed to praise you till after you were dead. After a moment, he said, 'Do they eat you?'

The Doctor's mouth twitched, but Robert could tell he wasn't actually laughing at him. 'No, they don't,' he said. 'Is that what people were thinking?'

Robert nodded.

'I can't tell you it's much better, though, what they do,' he said. 'People are still dying. Dying horribly. It's evil, what they're doing.'

Robert couldn't help himself: he choked, a hoarse cry sticking half in, half out of his throat.

The Doctor grabbed his shoulder. 'It's all right,' he said. 'I know it's scary. But I'm not going to let them hurt you.'

But Robert wasn't crying for himself. Finally, he had to think about it. 'They took my mum!' he cried. 'They took my mum and I hated her and now I'll never see her again and it's the most awful feeling in the world!'

He felt the Doctor's grip tightening on his shoulder. 'Number one, it's OK to cry,' he said, seeming to sense that the idea of breaking down in front of a stranger, and a hero at that, was almost as bad for Robert as the thing he was crying about. 'I cry all the time.'

'Do you?' said Robert through his tears, knowing that the man was lying, but trying to believe him anyway.

'Yup,' said the Doctor. 'Number two, we're going to talk about this, you and me. I've already had to have a bit of a chat to Rose – that's my friend, the girl who was with me –'

Rose – even her name was beautiful…

'– about people you hate dying. But I think we might find you're coming at it from a different direction. Like, how you didn't really hate your mum at all. Or rather, you did, but it was a complicated sort of hate. Like, maybe you loved her as well. But whatever, we'll sort it out.'

And Robert thought he might finally understand what it felt like to have a dad.

The Quevvils took them into a room. It was really dingy, like all this place, but to Robert's surprise it had a great big screen on one wall, like a telly. And even seats where they could sit down. Were they going to show a film? Surely this wasn't what had happened to all the others who'd been taken.

The Doctor sat down in a chair, and gestured for Robert to do the same. He seemed to have an idea what was going on. One of the Quevvils passed him a device that looked just like the control pad for Robert's new games console back home. The Doctor took it and held it in both hands.

A light suddenly flashed on a panel on the wall. Frinel went over to it and pushed a button. A voice came out of the panel. 'Is the controller ready?'

'The controller is ready,' said Frinel, speaking into the device. 'You will dispatch the carrier.'

'Understood,' came the reply.

The screen flickered into life, though at the moment it showed nothing but a fuzzy pattern, as if the television aerial wasn't plugged in. Then the picture came into focus. It was showing a view of a door.

'Just out of interest,' said the Doctor, addressing Frinel, 'I know I can't get her out of the Mantodean stronghold cos she'll explode, but what're you going to do if I just make her walk around in circles for a bit?'

Robert didn't understand what the Doctor was talking about. But he understood Frinel's reply.

'That is what this human is here for,' he said, indicating Robert. 'If you do not perform satisfactorily – then we kill him.'

FIFTEEN

Rose felt sick, dizzy and woolly-headed, and she wanted to shut her eyes and hold her stomach until the feelings passed. She couldn't. It felt as if she was encased in concrete, unable to move. Like in a nightmare, where you're trying to run but your legs won't do a thing. But she knew that she was awake.

Her vision gradually cleared, and the nausea more or less subsided. She'd materialised inside the Mantodean stronghold, or so she assumed. Unable to twist her head round, she could see only the door in front of her and bits of the wall surrounding it – but at least she could move her eyeballs. After a bit of concentration, she found she was able to blink too. She tried speaking, but could produce nothing more than a noise in her throat. Something to practise, though.

She wondered if the Doctor was seeing what she was seeing. Was he sitting in front of a screen, gazing at an image of that very door, those very bits of wall? She assumed that the disc on her forehead had some sort of camera inside, as well as the technology that enabled the Doctor to control her.

Suddenly, almost without her realising it, her right arm began to move. She didn't feel it at all, it might have been being pulled up by a piece of string for all the internal awareness she had. Her fist clenched. Was he going to make her hit something? Then suddenly her thumb popped bolt upright, at ninety degrees from her fist. She stared at her hand. The Doctor was giving her a thumbs-up sign.

All very well for you, Doctor, you're not the one doing a Lady Penelope in a pyramid full of deadly two-metre praying mantises.

There were symbols on the door, little touch panels that she could make nothing of. Luckily her arm knew what to do. Click, click, click, click, and the door slid open. Her legs took her through to the other side, and then stopped abruptly. Her head jerked down. In front of her was a pit. A pit deep enough that she couldn't see the bottom. If she'd been made to take just one more step further…

She tried to see where she had to go now – were there paths to either side? But her legs were beginning to tense up, her knees were beginning to bend… Surely he couldn't be expecting her to jump across! It must be at least eight metres wide. No problem to a giant praying mantis, but even Denise Lewis couldn't do that from a standing start! What on Earth was he playing at?

And then she was flying.

She didn't know how to describe it, and it was over before she'd even begun to process the experience. Something gave her power, the thing which had taken her limbs out of her own control had enabled her muscles to be exploited to their full potential.

It was monstrous, horrific, and totally exhilarating.

There was no time to think of it further; her legs were marching onwards, taking her down a dark, narrow corridor. There was a turning off to one side, and her body started to head towards it. Then an equal force started to pull her back. She stood in limbo, each force resisting the other. What was this? It felt like… it felt like the Doctor was trying to take her one way, but the controls wouldn't let him. It felt like a tug-of-war was taking place inside her, using her internal organs as the rope. She remembered bits that the Doctor had said, how there must be safeguards to stop people bumping into each other and blowing the fiction of the game. Perhaps the discs on their foreheads acted similarly to like poles of a magnet or something, repelling each other if they got too close. The Doctor had managed to override them when she and Mickey were playing the game in the underground base, and he must be trying to do so again. He wouldn't realise that it was hurting her.

She tried to say something, to protest, let him know somehow that she was going to be torn apart, but nothing came out.

And then it stopped. The Doctor must have given up.

Although, knowing him, probably not for long. Her legs started to move forward again. At the top of the corridor she had to turn a corner, which was scary – she couldn't peek round it first to check for Mantodeans, she was just propelled that way, unable to exercise any caution. Her stomach was in her mouth – but there was nothing there waiting to snip off her head. The Quevvils had given her a little gun, but she wasn't sure if the Doctor would use it – even as a last resort.

She came to another door, and her hands solved another puzzle in front of her eyes. The door opened, and her eyes went down again, checking for pits.

There was no pit, but there was something much worse. Fragments of a human corpse lay on the floor. She remembered seeing this sort of thing on the screen when Mickey had first shown them the game: they'd thought they were gruesomely realistic graphics. There was nothing left by which the dead person could be recognised, so by this stage it probably didn't matter if other players tripped over the remains of a previous game. Even with the few remaining shreds of clothing – in this case denim, maybe black cotton, once-white trainers – it would take a positive Sherlock Holmes to make any connection between some macabre image in a game and a person who'd gone off on holiday somewhere.

The metal forehead disc had gone, but then so had the head. Rose's head moved until she finally located the fleshless skull over the other side of the room, five or six metres from the rest of the corpse. The box of the disruptor, however, was still on the body, its bloodied wires looped around vertebrae and ribcage.

Rose's stomach heaved. She wondered, almost detachedly, if she threw up but couldn't open her mouth, would she choke to death on her own vomit?

Thankfully she managed to hold it down. It was just a dead body. It was pretty disgusting, but it couldn't hurt her.

But then, with a jerk, she found herself bending at the waist, her head getting closer to the grisly cadaver. What was the Doctor doing?! Had she been labouring under the misapprehension that they were friends, when he actually really hated her and wanted her to suffer? She could smell the blood from this distance, the faint whiff of a butcher's shop. Was he intending to do the whole *CSI* bit and examine the horribly dead body for clues? She could save him the trouble if so: this person had obviously had their head chopped off by a Mantodean's mandibles, and then it had been... eaten. Stripped bare. Oh, ugh. Butcher's shop was right.

She was getting closer. After a few tries she managed to shut her eyes, but that was almost worse. It felt as if any second she was going to plunge into the corpse face first. She opened them again to find that she was staring right at the skeleton's pelvis. And then her hand moved out...

Gross, Doctor, gross. He'd better have a bloomin' good reason for this...

And it soon became clear that he did.

Her hand touched the pelvis, went underneath, inside

the tattered remains of what must have once been blue jeans. The Doctor's sharp eyes must have spotted what she only now took in, a tiny black plastic corner sticking out from underneath. Her hand grasped it and pulled it out.

It was a mobile phone.

It was *her* mobile phone.

It was still on, transmitting nothing across thousands of light years. On the screen it said 'Home'.

These rags and bones had once been Johnny Deans, whom she'd known from school.

She had listened to this man's death.

Her hand switched off the phone, pushed it into her own jeans, and she was walked away.

'I want my mum!' screamed Robert. 'I want my mum, I want my mum, I want my mum!' Tears were streaming down his cheeks as he tore at the bonds holding him to the chair. 'Let me go! I want my mum!'

Frinel had left after helping tie them up, saying he had to ready the invasion force, and the remaining Quevvil had been staring at the screen ever since, but it now turned towards Robert. 'Be silent!' it shouted at him. It picked up a small silver box and waved it threateningly at him. Robert knew what it meant: if he didn't shut up the disc on his forehead would be activated, and he'd become a zombie like the others. Robert stopped his shouting. The Quevvil turned back to the screen.

Robert turned his tear-streaked face to the Doctor.

'Was that OK? Did you get it?' he whispered.

The Doctor answered out of the corner of his mouth. 'Yeah. Thanks.' Then after a pause, he said, 'Good for you to let it all out.'

Robert tensed. 'It was just pretend.'

'Yeah, right,' whispered the Doctor.

They sat in silence for a few moments, watching Rose's progress on the screen. Robert found it hard to fully accept what was going on, that what he was seeing was what the wonderful girl, Rose, was actually experiencing; that the Doctor was somehow controlling her every move.

Robert wasn't dead. That had surprised him for a start. What he was, was a hostage. That seemed somehow shameful: through him the Quevvils were forcing the Doctor to do things he didn't want to do. But Robert took comfort from the fact that he was actually managing to help the hero in little ways. The Doctor – as Robert had expected – had a plan. Unfortunately, both Robert and the Doctor were tied to their chairs, and this Quevvil had stayed behind to monitor the Doctor's progress. The Doctor wanted to do things without it noticing. Which meant that Robert had to try to distract it.

That had been the easy one. But the Doctor said he needed it distracted for a lot longer next time, and Robert really didn't know what to do. 'You saw it,' he whispered to the Doctor. 'If I do anything else it'll activate this.' He indicated the disc on his forehead. 'Then I won't be able to help at all.'

'So what you're saying is that we need to distract it before you can distract it?' said the Doctor.

Robert gave a half-hearted laugh. 'Something like that. I don't know what to do,' he said, and his voice sounded pathetic and whiny. He tried to control it better. 'I wish it had a disc so we could turn it into a zombie…'

'Yes,' said the Doctor. 'That'd be good…'

The Doctor negotiated Rose up a flight of steep steps. The Quevvil was now watching the screen again.

'Look at me,' whispered the Doctor. Robert did so. The Doctor leaned over and examined the disc.

'We've tried to remove them,' Robert told him. 'But we just couldn't.'

'You're not me,' said the Doctor, grinning. But then his face fell. 'Damn!' he said. 'I gave my sonic screwdriver to Rose. Oh well, improvisation it is then… Start yelling.'

Robert did as he was told. The Quevvil might zombify him, but if it was what the Doctor wanted…

'Let me go! Let me go!' cried Robert at the top of his voice.

The Quevvil picked up the silver control box and raised it threateningly.

'Quick!' called the Doctor, holding up the game's control pad. 'This thing's gone wrong!'

Robert and the Quevvil both looked at the screen. It certainly did look as if something had gone wrong – the picture was going up and down, up and down. Robert – but seemingly not the Quevvil – noticed that the Doctor was actually rapidly pressing one button with his thumb, again and again. 'Sorry, Rose,' murmured the Doctor. 'Still, bit of exercise won't do you any harm...' He waved the control pad at the Quevvil. 'I need this fixed.'

The Quevvil approached them. It leaned over to take the control pad. And the Doctor hit it, right on its snub, hairy nose.

The Quevvil reeled back, and the Doctor grabbed the silver box from its hand. Dropping the control pad, he prised off the top of the box, poked inside it, and suddenly pointed it at Robert's forehead. Robert jerked back in alarm, but to his amazement and delight, instead of losing all control of his body, he felt a tickling sensation around the disc, as if the little metal hooks were retracting from his flesh! A second later, the disc tumbled off into his lap.

But there was no time for rejoicing – the Quevvil had recovered from the blow and was staggering towards them, its quills straightening, ready to throw. The Doctor was still poking around inside the silver box. 'Quick, on its head!' he called out.

In a split second, Robert realised what he meant. He grabbed the disc and pushed his hand forward in one rapid movement. His palm slammed into the Quevvil's face, and he felt the metal legs push themselves into the monster's coarsely furred forehead. The Doctor had the top back on the control box, and pressed a button.

The Quevvil froze.

'Well done!' cried the Doctor, an enormous grin on his face. But Robert wasn't grinning. He was gazing down at his hand. At the sharp quills that were sticking into his palm. The pain was intense. He choked back a sob.

The Doctor followed his gaze. 'Ow!' he said in sympathy. Robert thought that didn't even begin to cover it. But the Doctor was actually looking serious. 'Got to get them out,' he said. 'They're barbed, and they can work their way in really quickly. If they hit a major blood vessel...'

Robert shivered. 'What should I do?' he asked, trying to keep his voice level.

The Doctor looked him straight in the eye. 'Can you bear some pain?'

Robert took a deep breath, and nodded. He thought he'd been willing to die for this man. He couldn't appear a coward in front of him now.

The Doctor put a hand in his jacket pocket, and pulled out a scalpel and an apple. He gave the apple to Robert. 'Bite into this,' he said.

Robert stuck his teeth into the apple, and held out his hand. There was a red-hot pain in his palm, and he crunched right into the apple in shock. He spat out the piece, and put the apple down. 'I don't think that's really helping,' he said weakly.

'One more,' said the Doctor. Robert felt another stab, and couldn't help but whimper. 'OK,' said the Doctor. 'All done.' Robert looked down, and found the quills gone from his hand. The Doctor was holding them, and even at a distance it was obvious that the barbed points had expanded outwards till they looked like miniature Christmas trees. No wonder the Doctor had had to cut them out.

The Doctor dropped the quills on the floor, and pulled a large white handkerchief out of his pocket. He began to bandage Robert's hand. 'Hold it tightly,' he said. 'But it shouldn't bleed for long.'

Robert nodded, gripping his palm as tight as he could with his left hand. But through the pain, he was happy. He'd helped! He'd actually helped! He'd helped the Doctor, and now they'd be able to rescue Rose, the most wonderful girl in the world...

He looked up at the screen, expecting to see exactly the same view as when the Doctor had abandoned the game a few minutes before. But to his shock, he found that wasn't the case.

'Doctor!' he screamed, too horrified to be embarrassed. 'A Mantodean!'

The Doctor spun round. There on the screen, the giant green figure of a Mantodean was approaching. Its jaws were open, coming closer and closer.

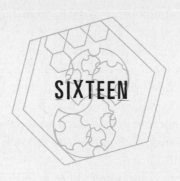

SIXTEEN

Rose's thoughts about the Doctor were not complimentary. She'd been suffering the indignities of being walked and jumped and run around, and now she was frozen in one place, like a musical-statues world champion. One foot was just off the ground – under normal circumstances she'd have overbalanced quite quickly. The Doctor was probably having a good old laugh at stupid, helpless, puppet Rose.

And just knowing that he almost certainly wasn't didn't stop her thinking about it. When she got hold of him…

She'd give him a great big hug, because she'd still be alive and he'd still be alive and he'd probably have saved her life, lots of other people's lives, and a planet or two into the bargain. And she wouldn't mention the helplessness she'd felt; how she hated this more than anything ever.

She wouldn't mention how she was worried she was

his puppet, doing things at his command, whether she could move by herself or not.

She thought she'd chosen to travel with him of her own free will, but she'd figured out that he had his own agenda. Because he needed a companion. He needed her. Somehow, she validated him. If a tree fell in a forest when no one was there to hear it, did it make a sound? If a Time Lord saved a world when there was no one there to know it, was he still a hero?

And she needed a hero right now, oh, God…

There was a Mantodean. There was she, stuck like a lemon in the middle of the room, and she could see it down the corridor… any second now – oh, help, it had seen her, it had seen her…

She tried to scream out with her mind, praying desperately that in a spectacular twist the implant in her forehead would turn out to be able to transmit thought waves to its controller. Doctor, help! Doctor, help!

Doctor – It was skittering closer, multi-faceted eyes examining this intruder in its path, this alien creature that threatened the security of its home. Not that she was doing much threatening at the moment.

As Rose watched, the creature's mandibles sprang apart, like a gardener whipping open a pair of pruning shears. If they were slammed shut, her head would fall to the floor as easily as an unwanted twig.

Doctor, help!

And then… her knees braced, and she was flying into the air, soaring towards the high ceiling, and her arms were reaching over her head –

– and she grabbed hold. Of what, she had no idea, she couldn't look upwards, but for all she knew her finger-nails were digging into solid rock. If she didn't know what she was doing was impossible, she wouldn't fall – like Wile E. Coyote happily running across thin air until he thought to look down.

Her legs raised up, and her head was pointing down-wards enough for her to see that the Mantodean could no longer reach her. It was scurrying about under her, prob-ably very annoyed. She was just starting to feel – not safe, but some relief that she wasn't about to die that very sec-ond – when she thought about grasshoppers, and the 'hopper' bit of their name, and weren't praying mantises really like them, and weren't Mantodeans really like pray-ing mantises, and did that mean they could hop up high, say, ceiling high…

The Mantodean was bouncing slightly on its back legs – preparing to jump? It was right under her, it would grab her, bring her down, snip off her head…

Rose's hands stopped gripping.

They opened wide.

She fell.

She landed right on top of the Mantodean.

Rose expected to be hurt, but she didn't seem to be. She didn't think the Mantodean was, either, just knocked to the ground, probably a bit dazed. She found herself jumping to her feet, running away, leaving the giant insect still lying in the middle of the floor. Round a corner, over a chasm, through a door, into a tunnel. Is it a bird? Is it a plane? No, it's SuperRose.

The Doctor was back in control, and she was safe. Well, as safe as she could be round here, anyway.

'There,' said the Doctor, whose anxious eyes had belied his cry to the screen of 'Soon get you out of there, Rose, no problem.' His frantic fingers finally eased off the controls.

'She's OK,' said Robert, relief flooding through him.

'Not out of the woods yet,' said the Doctor. 'Robert, keep an eye on the screen. Tell me if you see anything – and I mean anything. Threatening bit of dust, anything.'

'What are you going to do?' Robert asked, doing as instructed but able to see out of the corner of his eye that the Doctor had levered the top off the console.

'Few adjustments,' said the Doctor. 'This thing's pretty sophisticated, but not enough, to my mind, not for what I need. Those Quevvils are good at this sort of thing, obviously, but they can't make this sort of delicate adjustment, not with those great claws...' He tutted. 'Rose won't like it, though.'

'You mean you're going to improve the controls? Make her do more things?'

'Yeah and yeah.'

'No, I don't think she is going to like that.'

'Nope.'

The Doctor seemed to have stopped still all of a sudden. Robert held his breath – had the Doctor heard a

Quevvil coming or something?

He risked the tiniest glance at the man, and what he saw in his face was frightening. Hurriedly looking back at the screen, he whispered, 'What is it?'

The Doctor didn't answer straight away. Robert tried hard not to stare as he got up and began to sweep things on to the floor, crash, smash. Robert was terrified the Quevvils might hear the noise, terrified the Doctor might break something important; most of all, terrified of the Doctor.

'How dare they!' the Doctor yelled, thumping the wall with his fist. 'How dare they make me do this to her! Rose is not a toy!'

'She'll understand,' Robert ventured after a moment, scared of making things worse, but knowing he had to say something. 'She'll know you had to do it, why you had to do it.'

The Doctor didn't seem to hear him. His voice was calmer now, but icier; scarier. 'You don't treat someone like that. You don't treat a person like that. And they're making me do it, making me degrade her like that. We'll get out of this, won't dwell on it, won't ever mention it again. But, back of our minds, it'll always be there.' He thumped the wall again, then, after a frozen second, sat back down and picked up the controller. 'I'll just get on with augmenting my friend then.'

'I'm sorry,' Robert whispered.

'I know,' the Doctor whispered back. 'Thank you.'

* * *

Rose had stopped moving again, and was trying not to panic. Had the Doctor abandoned her? Would another Mantodean find her? What was that pain… in… her… head…?

Things were moving inside her: in her mind's eye she could see fibres worming around, wriggling along the pathways of her body. If she was X-rayed now, she'd look like one of those diagrams of the nervous system, a million wires threading through her, and she could feel every one of them. Then – after only a few seconds, or perhaps a lifetime – the pain faded, but a feeling remained, swamping every bit of her, from a tickle in her throat to a tingle in her toes.

She started to move – involuntarily, as before, but smoothly, oh so smoothly – no longer was she a jerky string-puppet, now movement flowed like a ballerina swanning across a stage. An onlooker would find nothing risible in Rose's deportment now, though they might well be in awe of her grace and strength and speed. She was a gazelle, a cheetah, a wonder of nature. Pits yawned beneath her, and were gone in the blink of an eye. Corridors flashed past, barriers were breached as she barely paused for breath. If Rose could have cried for joy, she would have done.

'Wow,' said Robert, watching the features of the Mantodean stronghold flash past, as if he was watching it on fast forward.

'Pretty good, if I do say so myself,' said the Doctor.

He'd switched off his anger, pushed it back – was concentrating on the job at hand, not what it meant. 'Lot of wasted potential, the human body. Right, time to get to work. I'm gonna be keeping a close eye on Rose –' his eyes didn't leave the screen at all while he was talking – 'so I'm going to be relying on you, Robert.'

Robert swelled with pride inside.

'First, you need to get us untied.'

Robert set to work. Their bonds were made of plastic and were tough, but now there was no watchful Quevvil waiting to pounce, he was able to set to and attack them with vigour. With the help of the Doctor's scalpel, they were both soon free.

'Now, you need to search around a bit. I'm hoping there's a sort of map thing, a plan, diagram, anything that looks like that.'

Robert began to explore the room. He felt nervous going past the frozen Quevvil – what if it came back to life just as he was in front of it? But he took deep breaths, and the monster remained statue-like, latest exhibition in the Chamber of Horrors, an expression of what might be shock still stuck on its hairy face.

On the wall behind them, he uncovered what the Doctor wanted. It was a bit like a tube map, only loads more complicated, all spaghetti lines twisting and turning and intersecting each other. Here and there tiny coloured lights blinked, some blue, some white. The white ones were moving along spaghetti strands, one noticeably faster than the others, while the blue remained immobile.

As Robert watched, a white light became still, and changed to blue. A few moments later, another blue light flickered and disappeared.

'That's it,' said the Doctor, looking quickly around before turning back to the screen. 'Brilliant. Now for stage – how many stages have we had so far? Stage whatever of the plan.'

Rose soared over a Mantodean, the poor misguided creature having had the idea that stalking towards her with its jaws open would somehow worry her. Catch me if you can, she thought, leaping ever higher and faster.

She reached the top of a series of stone steps, and there she finally stopped, gliding to a graceful halt. She wasn't out of breath; she didn't ache or have a stitch. Technology like this, and they use it to further a war. Just went to show how people could be clever and yet have no brains at all.

Her hand went to her pocket – and pulled out her recently retrieved mobile phone. Her other hand started to press its keys. It scrolled through the address book. It stopped at a name. It pressed 'dial'. It held up the phone to Rose's ear.

Mickey jumped when his mobile rang. To his astonishment, the display told him that it was Rose calling. He clicked it on hurriedly. 'Hello? Rose?'

Rose's voice said, 'Hello, this is the Doctor.'

Mickey took the phone away from his ear and looked at it. It still said 'Rose'. That'd definitely been a female voice. Rose's voice.

'You don't sound yourself, Doctor,' he said. 'D'you have some sort of accident?'

'You're probably a bit surprised,' the voice said. 'Or more likely you've just tried to be witty. Rose can hear you but I can't, and she can't answer back, so you might as well just shut up and listen. I need you to do something. It's really important, and unfortunately I don't have anyone else I can ask.'

'Thanks a lot,' Mickey muttered, convinced by the rudeness that this really was the Doctor, who was for some reason using Rose's voice to speak to him. And further than that, he really didn't want to speculate.

'Now,' continued the Doctor, 'I hope you're better at playing *Death to Mantodeans* than you seemed, cos believe me, you're gonna have to play like you've never played before…'

Rose listened to herself in some amazement as she outlined the plan. Her mouth was opening and her tongue was going up and down and words were coming out, and she couldn't do a thing about it. It was totally and utterly freaky.

And she seemed to have developed a northern accent.

Mickey was feeling slightly stunned. It was one thing to get a phone call from your ex-girlfriend, it was quite another to get a call from her new man using her vocal cords to speak to you, or something, and it was yet another thing entirely for him/her to casually drop into the conversation that she's – he's – calling from another planet, and needs your help to save the world again. Or a world, anyway, he wasn't too sure about that. All he knew was that the plan the Doctor had outlined was not only impossible, as well as bordering on the insane, but practically speaking totally difficult because it involved him having a telly, which he didn't any more. That actually felt like a far more insurmountable problem than the loony saving-the-world bits. It was getting latish now, nearly eleven, he'd have to find someone who'd let him come in and play a dozen games of *Death to Mantodeans* without asking awkward questions. If Jackie had been home he'd have had a chance – after the lecture about disturbing her beauty sleep… Maybe he could break in to Rose's flat – but if he got caught, the police wouldn't listen, they'd lock him up, and then who'd save the world?

A thought struck him. There was a telly at the youth club. The club was supposed to shut at ten, but Bob, who ran it, let some of the older lads hang out for longer if it wasn't a school night. Worth a go.

Mickey bundled all the games consoles into Mrs Burton's shopping basket on wheels, and limped off. The stairs were a bit of an ordeal, especially with the basket thumping down behind him, but he made it eventually.

As he headed down to the youth club, Mickey threw a quick glance up behind him, at Rose's flat. The windows were dark, of course.

The youth club windows were dark too, but he could

hear something from inside. He tried the door – locked – then knocked, loud enough to be heard, not loud enough to wake up anyone nearby.

The noise inside stopped abruptly, but no one came to the door. Mickey knocked again, a bit louder. Still nothing. 'Come on, open up,' he called, still trying for an impossible combination of loud and hushed. 'It's Mickey Smith.'

After a few moments, he heard a key turn in the lock, and the door swung open a crack. A pair of defiant eyes stared back at Mickey. He recognised the face: it belonged to a lad called Jason Jones. Mickey thought it quite unlikely that Jason had permission to be here, especially considering he was accompanied by a distinct whiff of cigarettes and alcohol fumes.

Mickey pushed his way in. Jason shut the door, and sulkily followed Mickey into the main room. 'What d'you want anyway, Mickey?' he said. Mickey knew he commanded some slight grudging respect round here, as an older, car-owning guy who had, at least for a while, been going out with by far the most attractive girl on the estate. Further kudos derived from his having been suspecting of murdering her, even though it'd turned out that he hadn't. Mickey had heard whispers that he had a gun collection, a knife collection, and several dismembered blondes under his floorboards.

There were two other lads in the main room, sat in front of the telly. Mickey recognised both of them. And to his horror, they weren't all he recognised. There, frozen on the screen, was a distinct image from *Death to Mantodeans*. Not the training level, the real thing. Mickey waited till the two of them had swung round to face him before answering Jason's question. 'I want use of that telly, and your help. Does Bob know you're here?' he carried on before they could react. 'And does your mum know you're sitting here with a can of lager and a fag?' he said to Anil Rawat, who nearly dropped his drink in fright. Mickey waited till all three heads had been shaken. 'Well, if you want it to stay that way…'

They clearly did. Mickey took the empty chair in front of the telly, and Jason pulled up another one. Mickey held out a hand and the third lad, Kevin, passed him the control pad for the game.

'It's your lucky night,' said Mickey. 'Cos we've got a lot of games to play…' He pulled out his mobile, and began to call Rose.

The Doctor asked Robert to watch the tube map thing as he continued to play the game. After a while, Robert noticed something. As the Doctor made Rose turn right, the fastest of the white lights would turn right too. If Rose was going straight ahead, the same light would go straight ahead.

'How many white lights altogether?' the Doctor asked.

'Six,' said Robert. 'Four of them are quite near the outside. One's further in, and Rose is furthest of all.'

'So they're the active players,' said the Doctor. 'The ones near the outside will be games that haven't long started. That'll be Darren Pye and the others, I reckon.'

'Mr Snow and Mr and Mrs Nkomo,' said Robert. 'What about the other one?'

'A game that was already being played,' said the Doctor. 'Could be

your mum

anyone.'

'What about the blue lights?' Robert asked.

The Doctor hmmed. 'You say you saw a white light turn blue, and a blue light go out?'

Robert nodded, then remembered the Doctor wasn't looking at him. 'Yes,' he said.

'Then I would think the blue lights are people in inactive games. They're standing there waiting for someone to move them again.'

'Or for a Mantodean to find them,' said Robert, who'd realised what it must mean when a light went out. 'And then…'

'I'm afraid so,' said the Doctor. 'Game over.'

SEVENTEEN

Mickey was getting everyone organised while he was waiting for Rose – or for the Doctor – to answer the phone. The Doctor had explained that because the only sense he was sharing with Rose was sight, he'd have to keep looking at the phone to check if it was ringing, so Mickey would have to be persistent.

There was a black-and-white portable in the kitchen, and Mickey had got Jason to bring that in. Anil had booted up the youth club's ancient PC and was connecting to the Internet, and Kevin was sorting through the pile of consoles that Mickey had brought with him.

'The trouble is,' Mickey was calling across to Anil, 'anyone who's playing the game won't be checking the message board. And we don't want to get anyone starting a new game. But see if you can find anyone anyway. No one should have got any games from alienkiller1984 yet, cos he won't have had time to sell them on, but warn people he's a dangerous loony or something, just in case.'

'OK,' said Anil.

Kevin had started to connect up a console to the portable television.

'You can ignore ones that haven't got past the training level,' Mickey told him. 'But if they have done, remember, you mustn't start a new game. Only find out if they've got a saved game that's still active.'

'Yeah, you said,' said Kevin. He pressed a few buttons, waited for the screen to come to life. 'Not this one,' he said.

'Try the next one, then,' said Mickey. 'Come on, lives are at stake.'

'Yeah, right,' said Kevin. Out of the corner of his eye, Mickey noticed Kevin's finger circling round his right ear in the classic 'he's a loony' gesture. Still, as long as they kept doing as they were told, he'd cope. He'd been called a lot worse. Much of it by the Doctor.

Speak of the devil… Mickey's phone was finally answered. 'This is the Doctor,' said Rose's voice. 'I hope you're paying attention. If you've found any active games, this is what I want you to do…'

Robert was still watching the map, his eyes darting between the six points of white light. Suddenly, one of them started to behave erratically, jumping first one way and then another. 'Got one!' he called to the Doctor.

'Brilliant,' the Doctor replied. He kept talking, under his breath, but Robert knew that the Doctor wasn't still talking to him, he was muttering the words he was making Rose say. 'Good work, Mickey. Right, I'm sending

Rose to meet your player. Keep doing exactly what I told you. If you feel resistance, you haven't overridden the controls properly. Rose, soon you'll meet another player. I can't undo the control disc on their forehead, not at this distance; once it's been activated one wrong move could make their brain go squish.' Robert shuddered at the thought. Thank goodness his disc had never been activated. 'What I hope I can do, though,' continued the Doctor, 'through you, using the sonic screwdriver, is undo the circuits that make people explode if they leave the Mantodean stronghold.'

'You hope?' said Robert, worried.

'I'm sure,' said the Doctor reassuringly. 'I'm sure they won't explode.' He carried on speaking through Rose. 'Mickey, you'll then follow my instructions from before. But you've gotta find all the other people in there too.' He turned to Robert. 'How many are there?'

Robert ran his eyes all over the map, swiftly counting up. 'Still six white lights,' he said.

'Six people moving around,' the Doctor said. 'One of them's you, Rose.'

'Eight blue lights,' said Robert. As he watched, another of them was suddenly snuffed out. 'Seven,' he said. 'Seven blue lights. Someone else's just died.'

The Doctor reached back and squeezed Robert's shoulder. 'Seven people stuck here and there,' he said, telling Rose and Mickey. 'That's paused games, Mickey. That's people in trouble. You've gotta find them. That's twelve lives in your hands.'

* * *

'So, no pressure,' muttered Mickey, staring at the screen in front of him. It showed a tunnel. Hard to believe that someone was really in that tunnel; harder to believe that the life of whoever it was depended on him right now.

'Found one,' called Kevin, who was still trying the pile of consoles one by one.

'Brilliant,' said Mickey. 'Right, reactivate it, jump the person around like I showed you, and then wait for instructions.'

'So… are we going to be getting the prize?' said Jason. 'The one for winning the game.'

'Yeah,' said Mickey. 'We're gonna be getting the prize.'

Things were starting to become complicated – well, even more complicated. The Doctor, who could obviously keep a dozen things straight in his mind at one time, was relaying instructions to Mickey for both the games. Mickey was trying to control the one on the main telly, and pass the instructions on to Kevin too. It wasn't working. Mickey's poor controller was ending up going round in circles. He finally handed the control pad over to Jason, and concentrated on separating out the instructions for each game.

Anil kept calling across bits and pieces from his Internet search, distracting Mickey even further. 'I've found one person who's playing the game right now!' he suddenly yelled, making Mickey lose his train of thought completely. And he couldn't even ask the Doctor to repeat himself. Still, the Doctor was obviously following what they were doing; he'd work out where Mickey'd gone wrong.

'Right!' Mickey called back. 'Tell him you've got some sure-fire cheat codes or something. Tell him to jump his bloke around a bit. Then tell him you're going to send him a series of instructions and he's got to follow them to the letter. Persuade him somehow, I don't care what you say.'

There was a ping from the computer. 'Instant message,' said Anil. There was a pause while he read it. 'This bloke says he bought his console from alienkiller1984,' he said. 'Well, sort of.'

'But there wasn't time!' said Mickey.

'Bought it down the pub,' said Anil. 'From Darren Pye.'

Kevin and Jason looked up. 'You didn't say Darren Pye was involved in all this!' said Jason, sounding like someone trying not to sound scared.

'I can deal with Darren Pye,' said Mickey, with the confidence of someone who's recently heard that the person in question is on another planet. 'Yeah, all right, he's really alienkiller1984.'

'He says he bought the console off Darren down the pub for a tenner,' said Anil, continuing to read, 'and then later Darren comes back, offering to buy it back for twenty. This guy refuses, and Darren tells him it's for really killing aliens, and he's going to make a fortune off the Internet. But he thought Darren was a nutter and wouldn't give it him.'

'Whatever, keep telling him he's got to do what you say,' said Mickey. 'You've got to persuade him to follow your instructions, right?'

'All right,' said Anil, sounding doubtful. 'But if he's the

sort of man who tells Darren Pye where to get off…'

'Just give it a go,' said Mickey.

'Hey!' shouted Jason. 'I can see someone!'

Mickey turned to look at the screen. There was a shape in the distance. As he watched, it became clearer, became an image of a short, slim, pretty girl with long blonde hair. She was holding a mobile phone to her ear. Rose.

'Here,' said Jason, 'that's that Rose Tyler! The one who –' He stopped, shooting a glance at Mickey.

'She's been kidnapped by aliens and forced to do their bidding,' said Mickey.

'Oh, right,' said Jason. 'What do I do now?'

Mickey turned his attention back to Rose's voice coming from his phone, and began to pass on the Doctor's instructions again.

'He says he won't. He's been playing all day and this time he's determined to win,' said Anil. 'He's going to be the first person to complete the game, he's going to get the prize, and if he really is killing aliens then that's brilliant.'

Mickey sighed. It was all getting far too complicated.

Rose was padding down a tunnel. The Doctor's words were still pouring out of her mouth, and she was trying to listen to what she was saying. Mickey was jabbering on about stuff in her ear – she'd just heard him tell someone that she'd been kidnapped by aliens and forced to do their bidding.

Tell someone the straight truth, and they never believe

you, she thought. They just think you're being sarcastic. Easier than making up a lie.

It sounded as if she was getting close to someone, anyway. She thought back to that afternoon – good grief, was it really only that afternoon? – and her and Mickey sitting in front of the screens in the Quevvils' base. The figures coming closer and closer. The sudden realisation. That would be her, now. On some screen, somewhere, she'd be a distant figure on a screen, getting closer and closer.

Rose's head turned. The Doctor was obviously searching for the other player. And she could see him now.

No – her.

The other player was a woman, a pretty black woman in her thirties, wearing a scarlet trouser suit. Her eyes were wide with terror. Rose wished she could call out something reassuring, let her know it was going to be OK, that she'd soon be out of here, but her mouth was still pouring out lefts and rights and straight-ons into the phone, and Rose could say nothing of her own volition.

The woman was getting closer and closer. 'That's Mrs Nkomo,' Rose heard herself say. Mrs Nkomo was getting closer still.

'Whoops,' said Mickey's voice in her ear, as Mrs Nkomo, eyes darting from side to side in alarm, ran straight into Rose.

The two players stared ahead as they were carefully positioned facing each other. Rose's hand found the sonic screwdriver and held it out in front of her. 'Don't worry, Mrs Nkomo,' she found herself saying, the very words she'd wanted to force out. 'We'll soon get you out of there. Rose here is going to disconnect a few things, then we're going to lead you out. Half an hour, tops, it'll all be over. Oooh, here comes someone else.'

Rose swivelled round. Approaching down a steep slope behind her was a middle-aged white man. 'Apparently that's a Mr Johnson. He's been gone hours. Lucky man, the Mantodeans must've missed him. Come on, Rose,' said Rose, 'let's get on with it.'

She was turned back to Mrs Nkomo, and the sonic screwdriver began its work.

Robert watched the map as two little white lights headed towards the outside. That left four white lights, apart from Rose, and six blue lights. No – five. Another blue light had gone out, another player had been found by the Mantodeans. He was trying not to think... Trying not to hope...

Not that he didn't have enough else to think about. Robert was calling out routes to the Doctor, as the Doctor, keeping his eyes on Rose, relayed them to someone called Mickey on the other end of the phone. Mickey, the Doctor said, used to go out with Rose, so Robert hated him.

'That's it!' Robert said. 'Both of them are out!' Mrs Nkomo and Mr Johnson were safe – well, safe-ish – at last. Thank goodness. Five white lights now (including Rose), five blue lights.

Suddenly there was a buzzing on the sort of intercom

thing. Robert jumped. His mind was so full, so busy, so concentrated on the ten remaining tiny specks of light-life, that he'd almost forgotten where they were, that they were in a scary room in monster HQ.

'This is Frinel,' said a voice. 'Gerdix, the carrier appears to no longer be approaching the centre of the Mantodean stronghold. Why is this? You will report immediately.'

Robert looked at the Doctor, hoping against hope that he had a plan. What had they said before? Something about Robert being there to keep the Doctor in line. He had a feeling the Quevvils didn't bluff, either. If they came in and found what had happened, it would be goodbye, Robert.

But the Doctor seemed just as taken aback as Robert was. He jumped up, giving the control pad to Robert and telling him to keep an eye on things – and hurried over to the door. There was some sort of alien lock on it, but the Doctor didn't bother with that. Instead he began pushing cupboards and benches and anything he could find in front of it.

'Gerdix!' said Frinel's voice again testily. 'Gerdix, answer immediately!'

The Doctor's actions had only just been in time. The door rattled as someone tried to open it from the other side.

Frinel spoke again through the intercom. 'Herryan reports she is unable to gain access to you. If I do not hear from Gerdix in the next thirty seconds, we will assume he has been overpowered. Extreme force will be deployed. All humans will be killed. Thirty.'

The Doctor and Robert exchanged glances. 'I'm not human!' grumbled the Doctor. 'I have already told them that.'

'Twenty-eight,' said Frinel.

EIGHTEEN

Mickey was still flustered. The panic stations of a few minutes ago had passed: Jason and Kevin had guided their players out of the Mantodean stronghold, and everything was plain sailing from then on. The Doctor had stopped giving him directions via Rose. But everything else had stopped too. Anil had stopped trying to persuade this guy to play the game the way they wanted, because he'd stopped responding to his messages.

There had still been a couple of consoles left untested, and Mickey had been itching to try them, fully aware that any delay could mean the difference between life and death for the person at the other end, but he'd had to wait for Jason or Kevin to get their player in place. Kevin got there first, and Mickey yanked out the connecting lead and plugged in the first of the remaining games. No go. He'd tried the next. The same. No stored game.

And so it had stopped, for now, until it was time for the last stage of the Doctor's plan. But he still had people's fates in his hands, which was hugely unfair. If he'd wanted that sort of responsibility he'd have become a doctor or a soldier or something. But he hadn't. Nobody had asked him if he'd wanted this. Rose had chosen to get mixed up in all this stuff, he'd just got caught in her slipstream, and they all expected him to just get on with it. Well, actually the Doctor probably expected him to fail miserably. But no one had given him a choice. Ask, 'Mickey, do you want to get involved in this saving the world stuff, yes or no?' and he'd say no. Who would? But when you're already involved, when you're in the middle of stuff, no decent human being could walk away. It really wasn't fair at all.

'Is that it then?' asked Kevin. 'Can we go home now?'

Mickey shook his head. 'Nah. We've got the real work ahead of us now.' But as he sat there, flustered and thinking desperately, he hadn't a clue how they were going to do it.

'Twenty-four.'

'What are we going to do?' yelled Robert. 'That thing –' he gestured at the Quevvil called Gerdix – 'can't answer, it's frozen!'

The Doctor looked at Gerdix. Then he looked at Robert. 'Control box!' he said suddenly.

Robert grabbed the silver control box, and passed it to the Doctor. The Doctor started poking around in it at top speed, speaking very fast at the same time. 'This has roughly the same function as the control pad, and if

I could modify that I can modify this. Wish I had my sonic screwdriver… There!'

'Fifteen seconds.'

The Doctor waved the box at the Quevvil. It gave a faint shudder.

'Reorganised the connections, like I did with Rose,' said the Doctor. 'I expect it's quite unpleasant. Poor Rose. Come on, come on…'

'Eight seconds.'

The Doctor kept jabbing away at the controls. Finally, after at least three lifetimes, the Quevvil responded.

'Five seconds.'

Gerdix sprang over to the intercom with a grace that seemed totally inappropriate in a giant porcupine.

'Four seconds.'

The Doctor kept manipulating the controls. The Quevvil reached up a paw and hit a button.

'Three seconds.'

The Doctor did something that looked extremely complicated. Nothing happened.

'Two seconds.'

'Ah! I forgot…' The Doctor twisted a knob.

'One second.'

'Frinel, this is Gerdix.'

There was a snort from the other end. 'Gerdix! Why have you not responded before? Why could Herryan not gain access?'

'There was a… a power surge. We temporarily lost control of the communicator. And the door locks. And the controller was unable to command his carrier. All power is now restored. All functions will revert to normal.'

Robert waited with bated breath. Would it work?

Frinel replied, 'Very well. We are anxious to see the carrier continue. You will proceed as planned.'

Robert grinned, and gave the Doctor a thumbs-up. The Doctor dropped the silver control box on the floor, and sighed deeply. 'Making me sink to their level,' he muttered angrily. He thumped the chair arm, and kicked out with a foot, knocking the control box away. 'This is too much! Making people dance around like puppets, making me take away every scrap of dignity of my best friend... I can tell you now, she won't be loving it. But I don't have a choice. Only way to get everyone out of there.'

Robert thought he was going to start smashing things again, even though the Quevvils were watching them. But instead the Doctor suddenly snorted, and Robert was surprised to see he was almost laughing. 'Hark at me,' he said. 'If I wanted to feel good about myself, go to bed with a little moral glow every night, then I'm in the wrong business. Come on, we've got work to do. Where's everyone at?'

And Robert looked back at the plan, and saw to his horror that there were only four blue lights left. The Mantodeans had claimed another victim.

Anil had, amazingly, been able to track down two more of the people who were actually playing the game now. He'd been coming up with some pretty convincing cover stories, and in one case someone's girlfriend had seen his messages while she was browsing the Internet, waiting for her boyfriend to ring her, and had texted him, only to find out he'd been playing *Death to Mantodeans* for the last hour. Someone else had popped online to check their emails, and found one of Anil's fake news stories that had been forwarded on by a friend. Mickey had his own mobile to one ear, and Jason's to the other, and was relaying the Doctor's instructions from one to Anil, back at the youth club, via the other.

Then Mickey had collected the lads' own console and the 'live' one they'd found earlier, persuaded (blackmailed) Jason and Kevin to go with him, and they were about to do something that wasn't sensible at all.

He hadn't been able to resist glancing up at Rose's windows again as they left the youth club; his eyes were irresistibly drawn there. But there were still no signs of life. He didn't know why he'd half been expecting to see something. Jackie was still in hospital, as far as he knew, and Rose was… elsewhere. But when someone had a time machine, you couldn't help thinking they might turn up even when you knew they were somewhere else…

But there was no blue box standing around. Rose and the Doctor – future Rose and the Doctor, or even past Rose and the Doctor – weren't here at all. It was all up to him, Mickey.

He knocked on the door in front of him. Jason and Kevin shuffled their feet behind him. They'd taken some convincing. Mind you, Mickey was nervous, even though he knew it should be safe.

After thirty seconds or so, he knocked again, louder. 'Keep the noise down!' came a voice from somewhere above. 'Some of us are trying to sleep!'

Mickey raised his hand to knock again, but then he heard something, someone shuffling towards them. The door was opened a chain-length, and a wrinkled face peered at them through the gap.

'Hello, Mrs Pye,' said Mickey. 'D'you mind if we come in?'

Once they'd got over their panic about what Darren'd do if he came home and found them there, Kevin and Jason had seemed pretty impressed at the way Mickey had persuaded Mrs Pye to let them into the flat. They'd been even more impressed at the way Mickey had commandeered the half-dozen or so tellies they'd found in a back room, especially as he'd even got Mrs Pye to point out power sockets where they could plug them all in. He'd then uncovered Darren's stash of games consoles. There were dozens of the things – he must have been round the whole area – and they'd gone through every one of them. And then he'd heaved the biggest sigh of relief in the world, because they'd found four more saved games.

'There's only six left to find,' the Doctor had said. 'Four saved games, and two more live ones.'

So, just the two live ones to go now. Mickey knew one of them was the bloke who wouldn't stop playing, but he wasn't able to tell the Doctor that. Anyway, though, that meant they'd found everything except one person still out there playing the game. Strange as it seemed, Darren

Pye had actually done them a favour by collecting up all these games. He'd probably got more of them with threats than Rose would have done with pleas, and that meant that most of the games were in one place.

Anyway, four more people were on their way out of the Mantodean stronghold. And that meant that maybe, some time soon, Mickey would get to go home and go to bed.

Rose had been busy with the sonic screwdriver. She had no idea how it was working – she had no idea if it even was working, but she hadn't heard any explosions, so she was hoping for the best.

She met up with another middle-aged white man – Mr Snow, she'd been told – who had a sort of glazed look in his eyes, not as if he was scared, just as if he was refusing to believe this was really happening. She'd worked the Doctor's magic on Mr Nkomo, someone called Anne something or other, someone called Tim Breeley, and a Japanese girl who must have been there for ages because the Doctor said his friend Robert didn't recognise her at all.

One more person was heading her way, her own voice had told her. And she hoped against hope that this was nearly it, that she could get the rescuing stuff over with, so that someone could get around to rescuing her.

There were only four lights now, including Rose; the rest had left the stronghold. Robert was worried the Quevvils would realise what was happening, but the Doctor said even if they realised people were getting out of the place, they'd just think they were getting blown up.

Now the last blue light had turned back to white – and Robert couldn't help himself from spinning round every few seconds to look at the screen. Now it was approaching the white light that was Rose. Now – turn around – there was a blur in the distance that might just be a person. Now – turn back to the map – it was getting very close to Rose. Now – turn around again – it was nearly there, any minute now he'd be able to see –

It was a woman. It was… It was Rachel Goldberg. Robert forced himself to smile. 'Mr Goldberg will be so happy,' he said. 'And she was really nice too.'

He worked out the route to get Rachel out of the stronghold, and the Doctor relayed his words, through Rose, to this Mickey back on Earth. Robert kept a close eye on the remaining two non-Rose lights, but they showed no signs of doing the little jumping-around thing that the Doctor had worked out as a signal. The Doctor had Rose sever the connection to Earth, telling Mickey he'd call back when – if – they were needed.

'Rose,' said the Doctor, speaking out loud the words he was creating through her, 'there're still two other people in there, playing the game. I hope Mickey's trying to find their controllers, but we're running out of time. I'm going to send you to intercept them if I can. Maybe you can carry them out or something. But somehow we've got to get everyone out of there. I've got a plan.'

Robert inwardly cheered. The Doctor still had a plan!

'But everyone's gotta be out of there. We –'

'Gerdix! The carrier is not following the correct path! Have you had further power problems?'

Robert jumped as the voice boomed out of the intercom. 'Quick!' he cried to the Doctor. 'You've got to make him answer again!'

The Doctor was scrabbling on the floor, searching for the silver control box. 'I dropped it about here…'

'You kicked it away,' Robert reminded him.

'Must be somewhere over here…'

'Gerdix! Answer! If you do not answer within thirty seconds…'

'Here we go again,' said the Doctor. 'Ah! It must've gone under that workbench.'

Robert grabbed the game control pad and took charge of watching the screen for Mantodeans, while the Doctor crawled across the floor on his hands and knees.

'Twenty-five seconds…'

'No – where is the blasted thing? Aha!'

A Mantodean came on the screen. Robert instinctively pressed the button to fire at it. He imagined Rose's arm shooting up, her finger on the trigger of a gun… The Mantodean barely staggered as the laser beam hit it, it certainly didn't fall. Guns had pretty much been useless against them, Robert remembered from his own days playing *Death to Mantodeans*. He jabbed at the controls, hoping that the Doctor's improvements would help him out here. 'Doctor, she's being attacked!' he called.

As the Doctor threw himself back upright, silver box in

one hand, Robert made Rose execute a pretty impressive karate kick on the insect monster.

'Twenty seconds…'

Robert passed the controls back to the Doctor. 'You've got to get her out of there!' he said.

'Looks like you were doing a pretty good job on your own,' the Doctor said. On the screen, the Mantodean had reeled away; the kick had been effective. 'I think it's time for Rose to run, though…'

The Doctor guided her through a narrow gap, and set her running at top speed. 'Right, you take over again,' he said to Robert, passing back the pad.

'Ten seconds…'

The Doctor pointed the silver control box at Gerdix the Quevvil. Nothing happened. He shook the box. It rattled. 'Something's come loose!' he said.

'Can you repair it?' asked Robert, dizzy with the adrenalin of having saved – did he dare call it that? Yes! – of having saved the life of the perfect girl. Of even now being in control of her destiny. Of being in charge of her…

'Yes,' said the Doctor, prising the top off the box, 'it's just a matter of time…'

'Five seconds…'

The Doctor jabbed a finger in, restored a connection. The top went back on. A button was pressed.

'One second…'

Gerdix took a jerky step forward.

And the door of the room exploded.

NINETEEN

Rose was shocked when she found herself face to face with another Mantodean, amazed when she found herself shooting at it, and surprised but not unpleased to find herself delivering a hefty sideways kick to its abdomen. Forget Buffy, this was Rose the Giant-Insect Slayer…

She had been taken away from the creature, but then found herself standing still for what seemed like a very long time.

Then, suddenly, she spoke again. 'Rose, it's me,' her voice said. 'It's all gone a bit pear-shaped this end. I'm not going to be able to say much in case they notice what I'm doing. Can't let you speed along either, they'd notice that too. I can't get you out of there, not yet. If you don't carry on to the middle, they're going to kill everyone. But I'll sort it. See you later.' There was a pause, and then, as if he felt he should be signing off like on a letter, 'Love, the Doctor.'

And that was it.

She felt a bit aggrieved, because she was his best friend, and he was choosing to save the lives of all these other people instead of her – and although he wouldn't be the Doctor if he didn't, and of course she'd have said, 'No, no, save them not me,' if she'd been asked, the point was she hadn't been asked, and she thought it was perfectly reasonable to feel just slightly put out in the circumstances. The circumstances being her heading off to her probable death right now.

The door had exploded, and three Quevvils armed with laser pistols had kicked their way through the smoking remains. Two of them held their weapons on the Doctor and Robert, while the third went to the intercom and reported to Frinel. A few minutes later Frinel himself joined them in the room.

There had been some alarm when they'd seen Gerdix frozen in the middle of the room, one paw still raised just off the floor. Frinel had called in some sort of scientist Quevvil, who'd finally got the forehead disc removed. The Doctor had been muttering angrily under his breath while this had been going on, stuff about how they obviously hadn't designed the things to be reversible. Robert was more glad than ever that his disc had never been activated, but he was worried about Rose. Oh, and the others. The Doctor said that once he'd got his sonic screwdriver back, removing the things would be a piece of cake.

That was if Rose ever got out of the stronghold.

'What about your plan?' Robert had whispered to the

Doctor. The Doctor said that his plan would still work. Was still on track. His main plan, his big, important plan, the saving-Earth one. It was just the getting Rose out part of it that had hit a snag…

Frinel had said that it had been a mistake leaving the Doctor with only one guard. He would remedy that. Robert and the Doctor were marched out and taken to another room, a really big, important-looking room. There were loads of Quevvils there, bustling about, examining screens and dials and read-outs. There was a series of little booths that looked a bit like shower cubicles, each one lit by a muted yellow light.

A small Quevvil had carried in the Doctor's console, and was attaching it to one of the large screens. The control pad was given back to the Doctor.

Another door opened, and the rest of the humans were led in: Sarah and her mum and scaredy George and all the rest. Robert wanted to call across to the still-weeping Daniel Goldberg that Rachel was all right, but knew he mustn't. He tried to catch the man's eye, but couldn't. Then Robert was grabbed by a Quevvil and thrown back with the group. 'It'll be all right,' the Doctor said as Robert was taken away.

Frinel came over and spoke to the Doctor, loud enough for the humans to hear.

'You have not played the game as we instructed. You have attempted sabotage. You have attacked a Quevvil. You were warned that if you did not obey our instructions, the human would die.' He pointed at Robert.

Robert had been feeling almost detached from what was going on. He'd been worried about the Doctor's plan, about Rose, about getting the people out of the stronghold. The bigger picture. He'd almost forgotten about the threat to his own life. And here it was, all of a sudden. No wonderful heroic sacrifice. No taking a bullet meant for someone else. Just sudden, out of the blue, pointless death.

'Kill him,' said Frinel.

Mrs Pye seemed to have got it into her head that they were policemen – and although they say that policemen look younger the older you are, that's ridiculous, thought Mickey, looking at the two skinny teenagers accompanying him. She sat at her kitchen table, grumbling unintelligibly (she hadn't bothered to put her false teeth in), while Mickey, Kevin and Jason guided their charges across the many TV screens. Finally, Mickey put down the last of the control pads with a sigh. 'That's it,' he said. 'Now we wait for the Doctor. Jason, call Anil and find out how he's getting on.'

But Anil had had no luck either tracking the one remaining console, or persuading the other player to abandon his game.

'What do we do?' asked Kevin. 'Should we just, like, go knocking on doors, see if we can find the last game?'

Reluctantly, Mickey shook his head. Life or death decisions, he thought. He shouldn't have to make those. 'We stay here,' he said. 'The games aren't just on the Powell

Estate, they're all round here. It'll be like looking for a needle in a haystack.' He stared at the array of screens, all showing the same view; thought of the people poised at the end of telephones and email accounts, waiting for his signal. 'And the Doctor might call on us any minute, yeah? We've gotta be ready for that, or it's all for nothing.'

So he just sat there, staring at his mobile and willing it to ring, hoping that he'd made the right choice.

Frinel had ordered a Quevvil to kill him. Robert noticed, as everything became suddenly clear, that the Quevvil didn't have a gun. It was bristling up – he remembered the feeling of the quills in his palm, and imagined that spread across his entire body. If you had to die, it really didn't seem fair that you had to suffer pain too…

But the Quevvil had picked up a silver box, and was pointing it at Robert. Robert was puzzled. So was the Quevvil, as nothing happened. The Quevvil turned to Frinel.

'That one doesn't have a control disc, you idiot!' snapped Frinel. 'Kill another one.'

The silver box no longer pointed at Robert. He turned, feeling that he was doing it in slow motion, that it was taking him for ever. There was screaming: male screaming. Then the screaming changed to a sort of gurgling choke, as if the person was being strangled. Robert's gaze finally arrived and took in the scene. It was George; he was lying on the floor, clutching his head. As Robert watched, he stopped choking, stopped clutching his head, lay still.

Something trickled out of his ears; Robert looked hurriedly away again.

Frinel spoke to the Doctor. 'You were warned. From now on, the slightest deviation will result in the death of a human. Now, continue with the game.'

The Doctor's face had gone blank. Robert guessed he was feeling very, very angry and upset, and was trying not to show it. The Doctor picked up the control pad, and began to move Rose through the maze.

One of the Quevvils, who was hunched over a display of some kind, suddenly called out, 'The carrier is approaching another carrier again!'

Robert looked at the screen. Yes, he could just see a figure in the distance.

'Don't blame me,' called out the Doctor. 'I'm not doing it on purpose. I can't even tell where the other players are any more.'

Robert held his breath as Frinel waddled over to the Doctor.

They'd spent some time swapping Darren Pye stories – what he'd said, what he'd done, what they'd heard he'd done, who they'd heard he'd done in. It was quite a catalogue. Mickey would have found it ludicrous if he hadn't known for a fact that a good part of what sounded like scurrilous rumour really was true. But now they'd sort of sunk into an expectant hush, just waiting for something to happen.

Suddenly, the sharp ring of a mobile phone cut through

the silence in Mrs Pye's living room. Mickey jumped. This was it! But it wasn't his mobile, it was Jason's.

'It's Anil,' Jason reported. 'That bloke's got back in touch, the one who wouldn't stop playing the game. He says… he says he thinks he's discovered a new cheat code, cos he can see some bird on the screen. He's gloating about it.'

'Rose!' yelled Mickey. 'Tell him to do that thing, now! Tell him you've discovered a quicker way to the end, if he follows our instructions!'

'Did you hear that?' Jason said into the phone. There was a pause. Then Jason said, 'Anil says he doesn't believe him. He says that Anil's just trying to put him off, feed him a false route, cos Anil wants to finish first. He's going to keep on playing. He says… he says if that bird's a rival, he's going to nobble her…'

Rose felt as if she had ten-ton weights in her trainers. The Doctor was moving her at that slow, clunking pace again, each step an event.

Her head turned, and she caught a glimpse of a figure some way ahead of her. Brilliant! Was everything back to normal? But she had suddenly stopped still, she wasn't hurrying forward to meet it like before.

The figure was still coming forward, though, and with a start, Rose realised who it was.

Darren Pye.

She knew he was on the planet with them, and anyway the Doctor had told Mickey about it through her, but he hadn't said a word about Darren being sent to the stronghold. She wondered if the Doctor knew. Surely he wouldn't be so eager to rescue every last person if he did. She sighed. Yes, he would, he was the Doctor.

Darren was clumping towards her like a lead-booted ape. She instinctively tried to get out of his way, even though she obviously couldn't. When he got close, she was amazed to see that he was scowling. It wasn't that his face had frozen in an angry grimace, he was actually scowling. And there was more: every now and then he would almost pull back a limb, resisting the imperative placed upon him by the wires in his brain. He's strong, Rose thought, so strong. If he can fight against this...

She could tell when Darren had seen her, because his expression changed. His eyes narrowed, and the hatred directed at her was so intense Rose felt it like a blow. If she had been able to move, she would have staggered back.

Easy, tiger, she thought, as he lurched nearer and nearer. Now would really be a good time for the Doctor to do something. Because seeing Rose was only going to act as an incentive for Darren to really regain control of his limbs...

'The carriers should not be able to approach each other!' shouted Frinel. 'This game was designed so each carrier would follow a separate route! If the human controllers caught sight of the carriers...'

A nervous-looking Quevvil hurried over and examined the console. 'He has negated the repulsion field of the control disc, Frinel!'

Robert held his breath. Would they discover the other refinements the Doctor had made to the controls?

'Then change it back!' snapped Frinel.

'I… I'm not sure if I can,' squeaked the Quevvil.

Darren Pye was in front of Rose now. She couldn't help but stare right into his face. She could see every zit, every broken blood vessel, every snotty hair bristling out of his nostrils.

And then she sensed movement, and forced her eyeballs to look down, as far as they would go. Darren was raising his gun. Was it a superhuman effort on his part? Was it an instruction from his controller? And what have I ever done to you? Rose screamed inside her head.

Darren Pye grinned. His mouth opened slowly, and with an obvious effort he forced out the words: 'Baa baa beesh…'

Bye, bye, thought Rose, and braced herself.

'There!' cried the Quevvil, slamming the top back on the console and hurrying off to be as far outside Frinel's circle of awareness as possible.

'No!' shouted the Doctor.

It hit Rose like a bullet. Pain exploded, blossomed within her, till there was nothing else.

The impact threw her backwards. And that was all she knew.

* * *

Robert, watching the screen, gave a cry.

The man, the ugly man, had been pulled from view, as if he was on the end of a horizontal bungee rope.

The Doctor, not seeming to care that he was surrounded by monsters with spikes and guns and brain-squishing devices, started yelling at Frinel. 'How stupid are you? I thought the whole idea was to get her through to the end! If you've hurt her...'

Frinel appeared unconcerned. He gestured at the screen, which was showing a view of a rocky ceiling. 'The neural relays are still transmitting, therefore the carrier has not been damaged.'

The Doctor spoke through clenched teeth. 'She is not "the carrier". She is a person, and her name is Rose Tyler.'

Frinel waved this away.

'And even if she is alive, and you can just count yourself lucky, pal, that she is, she might still be "damaged". Like poles repel, an' all that. You switch that back on when they're next to each other, and what did you expect to happen?'

'Continue playing,' said Frinel, 'or we kill another human.'

'Oh, that's your answer to everything,' spat the Doctor, but he picked up the control pad again.

Suddenly one of the other Quevvils called out, 'Frinel! Mantodeans approaching!'

Robert swivelled his head to look. There was only the one screen in the room, the one showing Rose's point of view, but this Quevvil had a chart that looked like the one from the other room, only it showed a cluster of small red lights. They were approaching a single, shining white light.

'Evade the Mantodeans!' Frinel snapped to the Doctor.

But the other Quevvil interrupted. 'No, Frinel, they are approaching the other carrier. The one being controlled from Earth.'

Frinel waved a paw. 'Then it doesn't matter.'

'Doesn't matter?' said the Doctor. 'That's a human being! At least let me try to help them!'

'They are unimportant,' said Frinel. 'You will continue to play the game.'

Robert was still watching the chart. The red dots had now totally surrounded the white dot. And then, as he looked, the white light blinked out.

'Too late,' said the Quevvil.

Jason got a text message from Anil. 'He says the bloke messaged him. He says it's game over. He's blaming Anil, though I can't see where he gets that from.'

And Mickey's stomach dropped like a stone, as he thought, someone's just died. A human being's just died. And I should have been able to stop it. If I'd just thought of the right things to say.

Sod this hero stuff for a lark.

But, on the plus side, at least he'd got his telly back.

Rose, not dead, woke up. It took her about six seconds to remember where she was and what was happening. And when she'd remembered it all, she felt very, very cross.

Something bumped against her feet. She couldn't look to see what it was. Then she felt herself move. She began to stand up. As she did, she saw the thing at her feet. It was Darren Pye's head.

TWENTY

Rose had been taken away from Darren Pye's head, away from the Mantodeans she could see in the distance, chomping away at something unseen, but perfectly imaginable, on the floor.

She had been taken down many more tunnels, across chasms, up steps, and through she wasn't sure how many encrypted locks and booby-trapped doors, and she was really fed up.

Then, just as she'd given up hope of ever hearing another human voice again, she spoke to herself.

'Rose, it's me. You're nearly there, so I've got to risk it.'

Her hand pulled the mobile out of her pocket, and began to dial.

'Just got to speak to Mickey again. Listen, I'm going to get you out of there. Once you're at close enough range, they're going to activate the disruptors. I don't know what's going to happen then. But you'll be OK. Trust me.'

The phone was held up to her ear.

'What's that you were saying about being OK and trusting me?' said Mickey's voice. 'Is everything all right, Rose? God, I hope you're OK.'

But Rose couldn't answer him, and the Doctor couldn't hear him.

'Mickey?' Rose said, in the Doctor's words. 'I hope you're all set. Because it's going to be any minute now.'

There was an air of barely suppressed excitement in the Quevvil control room.

As soon as Rose had started the final approach to the centre, Frinel had ordered the Quevvils into the yellow-lit shower cubicles, which apparently were teleport booths. Nearly every Quevvil had squeezed in, leaving only one or two manning the various bits and pieces around the room.

Frinel himself was standing outside the nearest booth. The Quevvil called Herryan was in place to activate the disruptors, and then, the instant they were switched on, to teleport the Quevvils across to the heart of the Mantodean stronghold.

'I shall lead the charge myself,' Frinel had announced. 'It is only fitting.' He waved his fist in the air triumphantly. 'Final victory approaches!'

The final lock was the trickiest yet. Rose avoided the acid flow and the razor blades that thudded out at head height, while standing at the top of a sheer cliff, and finally cracked the code. Or rather, the Doctor did all that.

The door opened. A hundred Mantodeans turned to look at her.

'Mickey, now!' she found herself yelling.

'Herryan, now!' cried Frinel.

Herryan's paw shot out, and hit the button activating the disruptors. The screen in front of the Doctor went blank. Barely a split second later, the paw moved to hit the button activating the teleporters.

Robert felt his hair spring up on his head, the air full of static. There was a smell like lemon washing-up liquid, and all the Quevvils vanished.

The heads of everyone remaining turned to stare as the door of the room smashed to the floor. Through the doorway fell Mr Nkomo, Mrs Nkomo, Mr Snow, Rachel Goldberg, Mr Johnson, Anne something or other, Tim Breeley and the Japanese girl, propelled forward by their momentum, each with a disruptor strapped to his or her chest.

The yellow lights of the teleport booths snapped out.

Every screen, dial and read-out in the room died instantly.

And, for a moment, there was silence.

Then, 'I think all your mates have just been atomised,' said the Doctor to the two remaining Quevvils. 'It might be an idea for you to surrender now.'

Back on Earth, the one remaining player of *Death to Mantodeans* shook his control pad, tried thumping the games console, and switched the TV on and off a couple of times. Nothing seemed to work. He looked at his watch, and saw it was the middle of the night. How long had he been playing that game for? He realised he was really quite hungry and tired now. Plus, wasn't it supposed to be bad for your eyes? He'd get a sandwich, go to bed, and maybe try the game again in the morning. It might have sorted itself out by then.

And 100 miles away, a man who had agreed to pay £500 for something that would rid him of his wife once and for all lay tossing and turning in his bed, wondering if he'd made a terrible mistake, wondering if he'd been ripped off, wondering if the promised ticket would ever arrive, wondering if he really hated her quite that much after all...

Robert was feeling quite dazed. He couldn't quite believe that the Doctor had done it. 'Had to get everyone across the desert first, had to drag things out long enough for them to make it. Then split-second timing,' the Doctor had said. 'Those things only work at very close range. Had to be near enough to get here when the teleporter was still in operation, while the Quevvils were still streaming through the air as their component atoms – but not so soon that they'd muck it all up as soon as the disruptor signal was sent. Then we'd've just had a pile of angry Quevvils on our hands, and that'd be no good to anybody.' He'd smiled then. 'I suppose that Mickey's not so useless after all.' He put a finger to his lips, and hissed to

Robert, 'But don't tell him I said so.'

'But what about Rose?' said Robert, hardly daring to think about what might have happened to the wonderful girl.

The Doctor looked really solemn for a second. Then he gave a sort of half-smile, an 'of course it's all right, honest' smile. He looked round to where the Nkomos were hugging, and Rachel and Daniel Goldberg were clinging to each other as if they'd never let go, and Mr Snow was saying to Mrs Snow that they were certainly never coming here again, and they'd be writing a strongly worded letter to the company.

'I didn't know if the disruptors would knock out the control system,' he said. 'I thought they would – couldn't be sure though. Bit scared I was leaving Rose frozen solid in the middle of a bunch of Mantodeans. But she'll be all right.'

'But what about the bunch of Mantodeans?' asked Robert, who'd seen the screen in the instant before the signal had been cut off. He hoped that was all that had been cut off.

'She'll be all right,' the Doctor reiterated. 'But it wouldn't hurt to go and see…'

Every light died. Every technological hum cut out.

'Crikey,' whispered Rose. She said it to herself, in her head, but was astonished to hear the sound come out of her mouth. She could speak again! She tried moving a foot. Yes! She could walk again!

Her delight was slightly tempered by the realisation that she was going to have to get out of this room full of Mantodeans without any of those superpowers the control device had given her.

This room full of Mantodeans – who were all looking at her. 'What have you done!' screeched one. Rose was surprised. She'd never heard a Mantodean speak before, she'd been assuming they were just dumb monsters, beasts acting on instinct. How stupid she'd been – how could dumb monsters have created a maze like this, and puzzles and traps like those she'd encountered?

'You can speak!' she said.

There was a collective hiss from the Mantodeans. 'It talks! It talks!'

The Mantodean who first spoke stepped forward. 'If it talks, if it is not a dumb beast like the others, then it will explain why it has done this to us, before we crush its thorax and it can talk no more!'

'Hang on a minute,' said Rose. 'I… I think there've been a lot of crossed wires here. You thought humans were animals, we thought you were monsters…' This didn't seem to be going down too well, so she changed tack. 'Look, the Quevvils –' there was a hissing from the Mantodeans – 'the Quevvils have been kidnapping my people, humans, and sending them over here to get into your stronghold. They couldn't get in, but they'd developed this disruptor –' she tapped her chest – 'so they could knock out your defences and teleport in.' She looked around. 'Thought they'd be here by now. Although obviously I'm glad they're not.'

'You are an ally of the Quevvils?' snapped a Mantodean.

'No!' she said. 'They've been forcing us to do this. Really forcing, so we couldn't move for ourselves, or even speak. Look, it's nothing to do with me. Please, if I could just go, I'll never bother you again… I'm really sorry for what's happened.'

But the first Mantodean was coming towards her, and its mandibles were opening. 'You brought this "disruptor" into the centre of our stronghold!' it said. 'You have destroyed all our technology! You have brought all our defences down!'

'I'm really sorry,' said Rose, backing away, trying desperately to see if there was anywhere to run to. But the Mantodeans behind her were closing in. And the jaws in front of her were opening wider and wider, getting closer and closer…

Snap!

The Mantodean's jaws crunched shut.

Rose, to her great surprise, still had a head. The disruptor, however, now lay at her feet, the steel-strong straps now neatly severed.

'We shall study this,' said the Mantodean. 'We shall learn how to reverse the damage it has done, and we shall revenge ourselves on the Quevvils!'

The Mantodeans began to crowd round, legs and feelers reaching out to the disruptor, suggesting this thing or that thing to try. Rose whispered, 'So can I go now?' and began to back away again without waiting for an answer.

They were all distracted. She should really leave before they began to, for example, notice her again.

Wonderfully, the power loss had affected all the doors, all the traps and puzzles. She felt elated at first, thinking it was going to be a cinch getting out. But of course it wasn't. The power loss had affected all the lights too. The more she thought back to those hours wandering the maze of tunnels, and that was with the Doctor to guide her… and how on Earth was she going to get over all those pits and things in the dark? She was fit, and she was athletic, but she wasn't, much as she'd like to be, Wonder Woman.

She'd thought the adventure was over, but perhaps it was just beginning.

TWENTY-ONE

With indecent haste, while everyone was still trying to come to terms with things, the Doctor had dashed about removing all the control disks, and then sorted out the teleport system back to Earth – 'Can you fix it?' Robert had asked, cringing that he was making the Doctor sound like Bob the Builder – but 'Yes, I can,' was the reply, 'it's on a separate circuit, no worries.' And the Doctor had zapped everyone back to Earth. He'd then proceeded to smash the teleport controls with a large spanner.

Robert – who had begged, pleaded and behaved like a total brat to be allowed to stay with the Doctor – got a bit panicky, but the Doctor assured him he'd allowed enough time for everyone to rematerialise on Earth before he destroyed the teleporter.

'You'll just have to go home in my spaceship,' the Doctor told Robert.

And Robert wasn't going to argue with that.

* * *

Rose was inching her way very, very carefully down a very, very steep slope, when she heard someone crying. 'Hello?' she called out. 'Is there anyone there?'

The crying stopped, choked off. 'Hello?' said a woman's voice. 'Oh, I'm here, I'm here!'

Rose scrambled down the rest of the way. Her night vision was getting better, and she thought she could just see the dim figure of a woman. 'I'm coming!' she called.

'Stop!' the woman called back, turning towards Rose in a panic. Rose scrambled to stop her feet carrying on forward of their own volition. In the dark, she'd not noticed the pit in front of her.

She grabbed the arm of the woman. 'Thanks!' she said. 'I'd have gone right in!'

It looked as if the woman half smiled. 'Don't thank me yet,' she said. 'I think we're trapped.'

Rose turned round. Behind them was the steep slope. Hard enough to slide down. Impossible to climb up. In front of them was the pit. And there was no other way out.

The box might say 'Police Public Call Box' on the outside, but the Doctor told him that was just for disguise. It was quite a disguise! Because inside, inside the spaceship…

Robert thought his eyes were going to explode as he tried to take it all in.

'This is your spaceship?' he said. 'Really? It really belongs to you?'

'Uh-huh,' said the Doctor casually, but he gave Robert a huge grin. 'Brilliant, isn't it?!'

'And you and Rose…?'

'Travel round the universe doing good deeds, yeah. Well, and having a bit of fun. Sometimes.'

'So she's really… like, your assistant. Like Robin, or something.'

The Doctor snorted. 'Assistant? Rose, right? She travels with me. In my time machine. You'd think I'd be the boss, yeah? Yeah, right. There've been times I wouldn't've minded one of them little silver boxes, I tell you – it'd make things a whole lot easier…'

But Robert was no longer listening. His attention had well and truly been caught by something at the beginning of the Doctor's rant. '*Time* machine.'

The Doctor snorted again, but he was grinning again too. 'Yeah, yeah, I can take you to the furthest corners of the universe, I say, to infinity and beyond, and everyone's always, oh that's nice, that's good, but as soon as I mention it travels in *time* as well…' He flicked a switch on this amazingly bizarre-o giant glowing mushroom in the middle of the fantastic control room. 'Rose was just the same. And talking of Rose…'

'How are we going to find her, though?' asked Robert.

'Oh, the TARDIS'll manage, now the force field's down,' said the Doctor. 'I can't quite work out why, but she seems to have taken a shine to that girl.'

And he pulled a lever, and the room was suddenly flooded with green light. 'We're off!' said the Doctor. And Robert thought it was the most exciting thing that had happened to him in his entire life.

* * *

Rose was wondering if she could find a way of getting the sonic screwdriver to melt stone, so she could make handholds down the side of the pit, see if there were any exits at the bottom. It seemed a stupid, impractical plan, but it was the only one she had just at the moment, apart from the even more useless one about making a very long rope out of all their clothes. For a start, it almost certainly wouldn't be long enough, for another, they'd then be running around in their undies, and for a third, the flimsy fabrics probably wouldn't take the weight anyway. Shame it didn't tell you on the little label inside – 100 per cent cotton, wash at 40 degrees, do not tumble-dry, able to support up to 500kg.

Rose's new friend, whose name was Daisy, sat there quietly while Rose expounded her various schemes and theories. She still seemed rather shell-shocked. She'd asked Rose who else had got out of there, and Rose had told her about everyone she'd encountered in the stronghold. She hoped they'd all got out. Daisy didn't think she knew any of them apart from Tim Breeley. 'But then, I've been in there for a long time, I think,' she said. 'It stopped once or twice, but always started again.'

'You were lucky,' said Rose.

Daisy smiled sadly. 'Lucky? Perhaps. But that was everyone? They got through people very quickly. So no one else can have survived from the time I went in. I… I hope…' Tears were streaming down her cheeks. 'It was so hard, just me and him, his dad didn't want to know, it's been so hard making ends meet, but I tried so hard…

I loved him so much, and I know that teens are supposed to be difficult but he seems to resent me so much… But I'd have done anything for him, anything… And you try to protect them from measles and mumps and running out into the road and playing with matches, but you can't protect them from things like this, things that you didn't know about, things you'd never have believed were real…'

Rose sat down beside her and reached out for her hand. 'You had a kid?'

'My little Bobbles.' She tried to laugh. 'He hated me calling him that. "Mum," he'd go, "my name is Robert"…'

Rose jumped. She'd been so stupid. The woman had only asked about people in the stronghold, she hadn't thought to mention people back at the Quevvils' base. Obviously Daisy hadn't dared to hope he'd stayed there this long. 'Daisy, it's all right!' she cried. 'Robert's –'

But she was drowned out by a sound that wasn't just music to her ears, it was the most wonderful music ever, it was the greatest symphony ever written, performed by the best orchestra in the world. It was the sound of the TARDIS.

Rose had to grab Daisy, who had started to back away in astonishment and fear, forgetting – or no longer caring – that there was a very deep pit behind. And then, suddenly, there was the TARDIS in front of them, its flashing light banishing the darkness, banishing their fear.

The door opened. A young lad poked his head out – and saw Daisy.

'Bobbles!' she screamed. 'Oh, my darling, my darling!'

The lad put up with her massive embrace with fairly bad grace. 'Mum,' he said, 'my name is Robert.'

Then the Doctor appeared, still the same as ever, grinning away. 'Rescue party!' he said.

He turned to Daisy, and seemed to be checking her out. Rose coughed, pointedly.

'Is this your mum then?' he said to Robert. 'Funny, that. She's not really how I imagined her from your description…'

Robert shrugged and made a face.

'Hello,' said the Doctor to Daisy, holding out a hand. 'I'm the Doctor.' She grabbed at his hand with both of hers, thanks pouring out of her mouth. It took a while for the Doctor to extricate himself. Then he turned to Rose. 'There you are then. All right?'

'Yeah,' she said. 'I'm all right.'

They went into the TARDIS.

I couldn't have done it without you, Robert. You really are special. You really are a Chosen One. Some might even call you a hero.

Thanks, Doctor. But it was nothing.

Oh, Robert. You were wonderful. You saved my life, truly you did. Doctor…

Yes, Rose?

Are you thinking what I'm thinking?

I think I am, Rose. Robert – would you do us the very great honour of staying with us? Travelling round the universe with us? Doing good and having fun. That's what we do. That's what the three of us will do.

You mean it? Really? Me, travel with you? With you and Rose? Being the hero, being the special one? Of course I…

But there's your mum, now. Look how upset she was. And she'd know all about it. She might even want to come with you. You can't take your mum on an adventure. That's not how it works, that's not right.

And the Doctor won't ask you. And you can't ask him, because you couldn't bear it if he said no. You'd be so mortified, and 'mortified' does actually really mean 'killed' and you would have to kill yourself. And there's only the two of you, you and your mum. And you couldn't really leave her on her own. Not really.

Now the four of them were on their way back to Earth. Rose, the wonderful girl, seemed a bit quiet. He'd imagined her more happy, more bouncy. But then maybe she was, normally. Holding his breath, not quite believing what he was doing, he went over to her.

'Hello,' he said. 'I'm Robert.' Stupid, stupid! She knew that already!

'Hello, Robert,' she said, smiling and making his heart jump up and down like a yo-yo.

'Are you… are you all right?' he asked her.

She waved a hand. 'Yeah. Yeah, I'm fine. The Doctor's got rid of all that stuff from inside me, all the bits that went inside my nerves.'

There was silence. Robert desperately tried to think of something to say, something witty and charming, something to show that he was perfectly at home in her company and perhaps they could be friends...

He still hadn't thought of anything when Rose spoke again. 'Well, maybe I'm not fine. You – you had one of those things stuck on your head, didn't you?'

Robert told her that yes, he had. But not one that had been activated. Not one that had made him do things.

'It was horrible,' she said. 'Not being in control. Makes you think, though. Makes you wonder if you're going through life like that, anyway.'

Robert gaped. 'But you're going round the universe saving it!'

She shrugged. 'Yeah, right. But I'm only Robin. And I don't mean I have a thing for tights and underwear on the outside.'

Robert tried not to think of Rose's underwear. But he remembered what the Doctor had said when he'd suggested the same thing.

'Actually, I'm not even Robin,' said Rose. 'I'm more Lois Lane. He –' she nodded at the Doctor, who was busy at the console – 'gets to be the superhero. I get to be rescued.'

'That's what you think?' asked Robert.

'It's what I know,' she replied.

Robert grinned. 'Funny that he doesn't know it,' he said.

Rose's mouth fell open. 'He's been talking about me?'

'Might've,' said Robert, hardly daring to believe he was actually teasing the wonderful girl. 'Might've said a thing or two.' And still scarcely crediting his own courage in the face of extreme gorgeousness, he just laughed and refused to say any more.

They landed back on the Powell Estate, opposite the Chinese and the youth club, and Rose wasn't a bit surprised. The place was deserted, though – the latest of late-nighters had gone to bed, and the early birds weren't up yet. It was that depressing time in the early morning where the only people about were milkmen, police officers – and time travellers.

She explained to Daisy and Robert where they were. 'There won't be buses for an hour or two, I don't reckon,' she said. But Daisy said that was fine; they'd find a night bus, or they'd walk, or get a taxi, or something. Robert seemed to be about to protest, didn't want to go, but Daisy stood firm, and only a minute or two after the TARDIS had landed, the two of them were walking away together, Robert shrugging off Daisy's protective arm. Rose had suppressed a laugh, reflecting on how intensely irritating she had found her own mum only a few years ago. Well, and many days since, but in a different way. The lad had kept glancing back at her, and she knew why, so she smiled and waved goodbye.

They walked away together, the boy and his mum. Rose seemed sorry to see them go, so Robert kept throwing back looks, trying to reassure her.

But she couldn't bear it, and came running after him.

'Please don't go, Robert,' she said. 'Please stay with me. With us. It'll be great, the three of us together, being heroes out in the universe.'

And Robert wanted to stay with her, wanted to go back, wanted it more than anything else ever. But he knew he couldn't. So he said, 'I'm sorry, Rose. I've got to stay here. Got to look after my mum.' He smiled. 'Got to be a hero by myself, here on Earth.'

And although she still looked a bit sad, she smiled and said, 'I understand. You're doing the right thing.'

And he knew that he was.

He turned to his mum and said, gruffly, stumbling a bit over the words, 'I'm glad you're OK. I'm glad they didn't hurt you.'

And she gave him a look full of sunshine, lighting up the world.

Then together, happy, they went home.

Rose stopped waving as Robert and Daisy turned the corner and disappeared from sight. She looked at the Doctor and sighed. 'Suppose we'd better hang around till the morning then. Go and see everyone. Thank Mickey for saving the day, and all that. Make sure he's given Mrs Burton her shopping basket back. Stuff like that.'

The Doctor looked horror-stricken. 'Tell Mickey the idiot that he saved the day? What d'you wanna do that for?'

'You said he did! You told me all about it!'

He shook his head. 'No I didn't. Didn't say anything of the kind. I said he'd been of some slight use, and at least he didn't muck everything up like normal.'

'You could tell him that then,' she said. 'It's high praise, coming from you.'

But he looked quite alarmed.

'And then there's my mum,' she said. 'I need to call the hospital, find out how she is.'

She glanced at Bucknall House, up high at her flat.

There was a light on in the window.

'Mum said that Darren Pye nicked her keys!' she said. 'We've got burglars!' And she raced off.

Rose let herself into the flat as quietly as she could. The Doctor was following on behind. Burglars didn't stand a chance against them.

Light was coming from under the door to her right. Her mum's room. She pushed the door open, ready to shout or fight or scream.

But inside there was just her mum, asleep. The bruises on her face shone brightly coloured in the illumination from the lamp, and Rose's heart twisted.

She put up a hand to stop the Doctor coming any further, and padded softly over to the bed. But she must have made some noise, because Jackie's eyes flickered open. There was alarm in them for a moment, then relief and happiness as she recognised Rose.

'Hello, darling,' she whispered.

'Hello, Mum,' said Rose. 'They let you out then?' She hadn't thought they would, not yet. Her mum had looked so awful. But the sense of relief, knowing it hadn't been as bad as all that – it was overwhelming.

Jackie smiled sleepily. 'Mm. Said I'll be fine. Just take it easy.' She yawned.

'Go back to sleep,' Rose said.

'Will you still be here in the morning?'

Rose leaned over and kissed her mum gently on the forehead. 'Dunno,' she said. 'But I'll see you soon, whatever.'

Then, as Jackie's eyes closed again, Rose crept out of the room.

The Doctor was making a cup of tea in the kitchen.

'Mum's asleep,' Rose said, yawning herself. 'Not a bad idea, I reckon. I've got my room and you can have the sofa.'

The Doctor helped himself to a biscuit. 'Yeah, then maybe tomorrow we could go and feed the ducks in the park, or p'raps there'll be a good film on telly.'

She gave him a hard stare. 'So, you're telling me you don't want to hang around.'

"S boring,' he said. 'Who wants to do ordinary things like sleep, when there's a universe to explore? What would you rather do, catch forty winks, or nip off to have a look at the moons of Jupiter?'

'I don't know,' she said, teasing. 'Isn't it quite cold up there?'

'Somewhere warm, then!' he said. 'We could watch the building of the Great Pyramid, or investigate this rumour I heard about this mad scientist who tried to build asbestos robots to colonise the sun.'

And all of Rose's tiredness fell away as he spoke. She

looked out of the window as the sun rose upon another grey London day, and thought about the alternatives the Doctor was offering. And she realised that while she might truly be the mistress of her own destiny, sometimes there really wasn't much of a choice.

'Yeah, all right,' she said.

So, arm in arm, they left the flat, and walked towards the future.

Acknowledgements

Huge amounts of thanks go to the lovely Russell T Davies and Helen Raynor for being so helpful, generous, insightful, and just plain fantastic. Oh, and for bringing back *Doctor Who* so gloriously!

Justin Richards and Steve Cole, fellow authors and much-loved friends, have been brilliant, as always.

Nothing would have been possible without the support of my family, especially Nick, Mum, Dad and Helen.

Thanks also to David Bailey for invaluable technical assistance and boundless enthusiasm.

About the author

Jacqueline Rayner is an author and editor who spent nearly seven years working on the BBC's range of Eighth Doctor novels, but – although sad to see him go – was fickle enough to come to utterly adore his successor almost immediately.

She lives in Essex with two cats, and a husband who is currently nearing the final level of *Ratchet and Clank 3*. If either Ratchet or Clank is real and is reading this, please get in touch.

In 1920s London the Doctor and Rose find themselves caught up in the hunt for a mysterious murderer. But not everything is what it seems. Secrets lie behind locked doors and inhuman killers roam the streets.

Who is the Painted Lady and why is she so interested in the Doctor? How can a cat return from the dead? Can anyone be trusted to tell – or even know – the truth?

With the faceless killers closing in, the Doctor and Rose must solve the mystery of the Clockwise Man before London itself is destroyed...

The Monsters Inside

By Stephen Cole
ISBN 0 563 48629 5
UK £6.99 US $11.99/$14.99 CDN

The TARDIS takes the Doctor and Rose to a destination in deep space – Justicia, a prison camp stretched over six planets, where Earth colonies deal with their criminals.

While Rose finds herself locked up in a teenage borstal, the Doctor is trapped in a scientific labour camp. Each is determined to find the other, and soon both Rose and the Doctor are risking life and limb to escape in their own distinctive styles.

But their dangerous plans are complicated by some old enemies. Are these creatures fellow prisoners as they claim, or staging a takeover for their own sinister purposes?

Monsters and Villains

By Justin Richards

ISBN 0 563 48632 5
UK £7.99 US $12.99/$15.99 CDN

For over forty years, the Doctor has battled against the most dangerous monsters and villains in the universe. This book brings together the best – or rather the worst – of his enemies.

Discover why the Daleks were so deadly; how the Yeti invaded London; the secret of the Loch Ness Monster; and how the Cybermen have survived. Learn who the Master was, and – above all – how the Doctor defeated them all.

Whether you read it on or behind the sofa, this book provides a wealth of information about the monsters and villains that have made *Doctor Who* the tremendous success it has been over the years, and the galactic phenomenon that it is today.